Savannah Richards did not believe in chance.

But there he stood, head bent, focused on his iPad. Handsome in his black uniform - black tie, white shirt, silver stripes at his wrists. A captain's cap sitting atop his head His hair graying around the edges.

Noah wouldn't recognize her now – even if he remembered her.

He would be forty-two now. A far cry from the college senior who had been attached to her hip for a year. He'd been a boy then, but his features were the same.

A few pounds heavier, but that was to be expected. The five o'clock shadow that never failed to appear by early afternoon. The same brow that she had seen furrowed over a calculous problem seemed to have made a permanent home between his eyes.

No wonder, as he had worn it often.

Sometimes even as he'd studied her, though he thought she hadn't known.

BEGIN AGAIN

ALSO BY KATHRYN KALEIGH

THE WORTHINGTONS

Contemporary Romance

The Heart of Christmas

Second Chance Kisses

Second Chance Secrets

First Time Charm

Three Broken Rules

Second Chance Destiny

Unexpected Vows

Billionaire's Unexpected Landing

Billionaire's Accidental Girlfriend

Billionaire Fallen Angel

Begin Again

Love Again

Falling Again

Just Stay

Just Chance

Just Believe

Just Us

Just Once

Just Happened

Just Maybe

Just Pretend

Just Because

BEGIN AGAIN

THE WORTHINGTONS

KATHRYN KALEIGH

BEGIN AGAIN

PREVIEW: LOVE AGAIN

Written by Kathryn Kaleigh

Published by KST Publishing, Inc., 2022

Cover by Skyhouse24Media

www.kathrynkaleigh.com

Created with Vellum

To learn more about Kathryn Kaleigh, visit

www.kathrynkaleigh.com

Kathryn Kaleigh

1

Savannah Richards didn't believe in chance.

But there he stood, head bent, focused on his iPad. Handsome in his black uniform - black tie, white shirt, silver stripes at his wrists. A captain's cap sitting atop his head His hair graying around the edges.

Noah wouldn't recognize her now – even if he remembered her.

He would be forty-two now. A far cry from the college senior who had been attached to her hip for a year. He'd been a boy then, but his features were the same. A few pounds heavier, but that was to be expected. The five o'clock shadow that never failed to appear by early afternoon. The same brow that she had seen furrowed over a calculous problem seemed to have made a permanent home between his eyes. No wonder, as he had worn it often. Sometimes even as he'd studied her, though he thought she hadn't known.

As a college senior, the only time he'd left her side was when he was flying or training to fly. Sometimes she'd gone with him to practice on the simulator. She usually ended up using the time to study her own biology textbooks or read an English lit novel. Side by side, each lost in their own world.

The time, she thought wryly, had been well spent. After her freshman year, Savannah had immersed herself in her studies and graduated top of her class with a bachelor's degree in science.

Noah also had displayed a singular passion – aviation. And everything that went with it. Flying. Airplanes. Weather reports. When he hadn't been engrossed in aviation, however, he'd turned that singular focus on her. The memory brought a flush to her cheeks.

And a familiar stab to her heart.

As the terminal train arrived at the station and the door opened to allow people to exit, it occurred to her that she could take six steps to the left, get in his train car, and speak to him. It was a much more logical thing to do than just watching him – letting him breeze by her.

Two ships passing in the night.

No. He was a ship from the past. She would let him go.

She was still mad at him.

NOAH WORTHINGTON GLARED at the flight schedule displayed on his iPad and wondered if his lunch had not agreed with him. The terminal train at Atlanta airport was interminably slow. He wasn't sure if he wanted it to hurry up or to never arrive. He struggled to find a middle ground.

He was seeing an apparition. He knew it had to be a vision because the girl he recognized wore a snug red pencil skirt with matching suit jacket. Her black pumps, though, had a matching red bottom. She carried a black leather Louis Vuitton handbag in a cross-body style, freeing up her hands. He recognized the LV twist-lock on the front – its only readily identifiable feature. The silver on the handbag matched the buttons on her suit. And the gray of her camisole. Her long brunette hair fell in loose waves around her face. Her make-up was flawless down to the shiny, but muted glossy red lipstick.

The college freshman from his indelible memory wore jeans ripped at the knees, white canvas sneakers, and either a sweatshirt or t-shirt depending on the weather. She'd kept her hair pulled back in a loose ponytail. The only time he'd seen her dressed up was when she wore a dark gray cardigan and matching shell with black slacks to a dinner with his family. She'd worn low heeled dark gray moto boots. He'd been impressed, at the time, at how put together and cute she looked. Her hair had fallen straight to her shoulder and though he hadn't commented, he'd known she had taken the time to straighten it with a flat iron. Her hair was naturally wavy and thick and she hated it. Hence, the ponytail.

All in all, perhaps that was a precursor to the woman who watched him now. Or perhaps she was his mind's rendition of the girlfriend he'd so inconsiderately left behind twenty years ago. Besides, what college freshman gained no more than a couple of pounds and in all the right places after twenty years?

The vision watched him, though she didn't know he knew. He recognized the expression she wore.

She was still mad at him.

The train rolled in, the door opened, and throngs of people rushed out of the cars. She got into the car behind his, moving with that same lilt in her step that even he hadn't managed to dull.

She's only a vision. Probably some random girl from California who just happened to have similar – very similar facial features.

However, he knew the saying that one never forgot his first love to be true.

He glanced at the time on his tablet. He had time for dinner before his flight, now delayed, took off for Dallas. He didn't feel like going to the officer's club. Didn't feel like talking aviation. Or hearing about someone's new aircraft acquisition. He just wanted to enjoy some peaceful time to read his novel, order a martini he wouldn't drink, and have a meal.

He scanned his ID and slipped into the Diner's Club – away from the other pilots. He wasn't exactly nondescript in his pilot's uniform, but he'd learned over the years that the typical flyer tended to not bother the pilots. He'd never quite discerned if it was out of respect, awe, or fear. Perhaps just disinterest. Whatever it was, he'd grown to count on it when he wanted to be left alone.

He took a small table for two near the bar, his back to the room. He found it less distracting to read when he couldn't see people hurrying to and fro.

He ordered a sandwich and water. And resumed his attention on the novel he read on his iPad. It was about a man who never slept. In theory, he liked the concept, but in reality, sleep was one of his favorite pastimes.

And allowed the world to fade into the background. Which was exactly where he preferred it these days.

"I'd like a cosmopolitan," A woman at the bar behind him ordered. "with olives."

Who ordered olives with their cosmopolitans?

The server said something he couldn't understand. And the woman laughed.

Noah froze. Then in slow motion lifted his head and turned enough to see the woman in the red suit.

She had not been a vision. She was Savannah Skye Richards. His college sweetheart all grown up.

He'd recognized her, but his mind had refused to accept the reality that after twenty years, she'd be standing in front of him.

Closing his iPad, he laid it on the table and silently turned his chair around so he could watch her. He leaned back, his six-foot frame appearing relaxed – disguising the cat-like tension coursing through him.

She hadn't spotted him yet. Her gaze was glued to her phone – her fingers typing rapidly. The years had been good to her. She'd always been pretty, but now… she was drop-dead gorgeous. There was an air about her that hadn't been there when she was struggling in college. She carried an air of assurance and confidence now that hadn't been there before.

Twenty years. Then twice random crossings in less than an hour. It was more than he could ignore.

She must have felt him watching her. She glanced up, typed a couple of key-strokes. Then looked up again. He could tell by the way the corners of her mouth twitched the moment his presence registered with her. With her new self-assurance, he was certain that only he could tell. He'd spent, after all, countless hours studying her. For nearly a whole year.

Their gazes locked. He smiled. God, but it was good to see her.

Déjà vu was an understatement.

He'd been working registration his senior year. She was a freshman. Her first day on campus at Auburn University in Auburn, Alabama. He'd taken one look at her and fallen head over heels.

This time, however, instead of smiling, she was looking… displeased to see him.

He stood up, closed the distance between them, and sat at the bar next to her. "What brings you to this gin joint?" he said.

"Work," she said, clicking off her iPhone.

"It's been awhile," he said.

"Twenty years," she said, as the server set her cosmopolitan in front of her. She picked it up. Sipped.

"What are the odds?" he asked.

"I don't believe in chance." She kept her eyes focused on her drink.

"I guess a date at the casino is out."

She scoffed. "A date is out."

"Savannah Skye," he said.

"Savannah," she corrected.

He rubbed his chin. "Savannah. Look at me," She lifted her eyes and he saw a glimpse of the pain before she checked it.

"It's been twenty years since we saw each other. Let's at least say hello."

"Hello," she said.

"That's better."

She scowled again. "You started it."

He shook his head. "You're right. I did. I'm sorry. I was caught off guard."

She smiled, albeit a little wobbly. "I'm sorry, too. I've seen you twice in one day. That can't be coincidence."

"I agree," he said. "You look good. You look like I imagined."

She raised an eyebrow. "You imagined me."

He chuckled. "On occasion, yes."

"You're married," she pointed out, nodding toward his ring finger.

He glanced down. Saw the line on his ring finger, no more than a shadow to most. She always had been observant. "Divorced. Separated actually."

"Right," she said, looking at him askance. "Aren't you all?"

"What?"

She shrugged.

"It seems you've been hanging around the wrong crowd."

"Is that so? When's your divorce hearing date?"

"I don't know."

She rolled her eyes. Sipped her drink.

"Seriously. It's uncontested. I'm not even sure we have to go."

She glanced at him. Unlocked her phone.

"Ok. Here," he said, taking his own phone out of his pocket. "Let's call Matthew. Let's call my attorney."

"Let's don't."

"Why are you so interested in my marital state?"

"Ok, let's say for now I believe you."

"No, really, why are you?"

Her gaze met his now. She chuckled. "You've already asked me out."

"I most certainly did not."

"The casino," she said, locking her phone again.

He shook his head, "It's a figure of speech. When did you become so literal?"

She leaned back. Sighed. "After being hit on about five hundred times."

"Admirable," he said, "I can see the attraction."

She laughed. "Not like that. As part of my job."

He considered her in a different light now. Her clothes were much too fine for a stripper. Definitely not a prostitute.

"You're an escort?"

She sighed. "I see you never developed a filter."

He shrugged. "Some things never change."

"I'm not a call girl." She glared at him. "Or a prostitute. So don't get any ideas."

"I think you're about twenty-one years late on that request."

"Yeah, well, you're married now."

"Separated."

"Same thing."

"You're difficult. I'm impressed. What about you?"

He'd yet to get a glimpse of her ring finger. Truthfully, he'd been too enthralled to even think to look.

She held up her unadorned hand.

"Divorced?"

"Never married."

"Are you telling me that you never…" He trailed off. This

conversation was completely unfair. He had no way to know what damage he'd done to her all those years ago.

"I work a lot."

He nodded. Self-sufficient. Successful. Hence the air of confidence. "What kind of work?"

"I'm a drug rep."

"Really?" Not at all what he expected.

"You may recall I was a science major."

"I do recall. And I'm sure you excelled."

"You could say that."

He smiled to himself. She had that slightly pouty expression that had always worked on him.

"I'm a pilot," he said, before he could stop himself.

She laughed. A genuine laugh now. Her green eyes twinkled with sincerity.

And it was in that moment. Just like that, that the years fell away and he was that college senior all over again. In love with the freshman coed.

"I never would have guessed."

"Did the uniform give me away?"

"That and the unerring devotion you put toward achieving that goal."

He sat a little taller in his chair. "You're successful at this drug rep thing you do," he said.

She tilted her head with a little smile. "I suppose. Why would you say that?"

"Because you're good at everything you do and…" he lifted one eyebrow suggestively. "You have a way of making a man do whatever it is you want."

She shook her head. The smile disappeared back into the little pout. "That seems a little odd coming from you." A silent message appeared on her phone. She checked it and pushed her unfinished drink aside.

"I'm sorry," she said.

She had managed to do it again. She had mesmerized him and he had no idea what she was talking about. "Sorry about what?"

"I have to go."

"Go?" He checked his watch. Such a short time had passed since he'd come into the club… yet his life, it seemed, had been altered forever.

The girl he had spent twenty years wondering about. Twenty years with a love in his heart that hadn't died.

And here she was. In the flesh.

"Yes," she said, with the flash of a smile at the corner of her lips. "I have a flight to catch." She stood up.

"Of course you do." *Why else would she be here?* For a mere moment in time, he'd allowed himself to think that she was there in his world just for him. Just for him and no one else.

She stood up. Pushed her chair to the bar. "It was good to see you again, Noah," she said, her lips curved in a polite smile no doubt used successfully when working with doctors.

"It was good to see you, too," he said, automatically.

She held out her hand.

He took her hand, but didn't shake it as she had obviously intended, but held it. Stared into those mesmerizing green eyes. She pulled back almost imperceptibly. He held tighter. Felt a gut-wrenching juxtaposition of familiar and new as she gave in and squeezed back. Just for a moment.

A moment in time. When his heart was light and the world narrowed down to them. Just the two of them.

"I'm gonna miss my flight," she said, pulling back in earnest now.

He released her. "Go," he said.

She picked up her bag and turned. Took a step.

His heart sank. Heavy again.

"Wait," he said, out of his chair in a flash and closing the distance between them. Stepping in front of her.

She raised an eyebrow.

"How will I find you?"

Her lips curved into a smug little smile. The smile he'd seen her wear after she aced a chemistry exam. "Perhaps we'll bump into each other again," she said.

"No," he insisted. "It's been twenty years. We both travel all the time. Right? You travel?"

"A fair amount."

"Well, you don't believe in chance. Yet in one day, we've bumped into each other twice... in one hour."

She shrugged. "What are the odds?"

He scoffed. "Out of the mouth of the one who doesn't believe in chance."

"I believe in science."

"Well, scientifically, we could never see each other again."

"You could always look for me this time."

He absorbed the jab. Owned it. "I could. I will. But the world is a big place."

She seemed to consider. Squinted into his eyes. Searching for something only she knew to look for.

"New York."

"New York what?"

"I'll be in New York for the next five days."

"Ha. New York doesn't narrow the world by very much."

She nodded. "It is a big city. But you know enough about me to find me."

"Wait," he said. "Until Monday?"

"Tuesday."

"Come on," he said. She turned. Smiled over her shoulder. That smile that had once been reserved only for him.

"See you around," she said, and walked away from him. He watched her walk through the door.

And took a deep steadying breath. Glanced at his watch.

Now was not the time for a panic attack. He had a plane to fly in less than an hour.

SAVANNAH RUSHED DOWN THE CORRIDOR. She could not afford to miss this flight, but she wasn't late.

She wasn't thinking straight. Her blood pounded in her ears. She'd only known that she had to get away. Before her composure shattered.

Noah Worthington had been the last person she had expected to see today. When he'd disappeared out of her life twenty years ago, she'd waited for him. She'd waited longer than she cared to admit, even to herself. She hadn't dated any one else in college. She'd gone into a dating moratorium after he left. Then, after graduation, she'd gone through a phase of serial relationships until ending up in a five-year engagement that had ended four years ago. She'd gone back into her no dating phase with the exception of a couple of dinners here and there. She'd never even signed up for a dating website service.

It was like Noah had taken it all out of her.

She took a seat in the waiting area and found herself studying the pilots as they, too, waited for the plane to arrive.

She wondered again, as she often had while raking in frequent flyer miles, what kind of life they had. Even though they were a little like taxi drivers, as Noah had so oddly pointed out to her so many years ago, they had professionalism and respect and an aloofness from the rest of the world.

Very few were invited into their worlds. Flight attendants seemed to have the most direct route. From her view in first class flight, she'd watched a romance or two unfold between pilots and flight attendants. She had yet to see anything more than cordial interaction between pilots and passengers. And to think that she'd been a part of that world once. At least to some extent. She'd been on the ground floor of a pilot in training.

Did their wives feel part of their world? Or did they feel like they perched on the fringe of an elite group? Only the elite group got to travel around the world with the lives of innocents in their hands.

As she allowed her musings to keep her from thinking directly about Noah, a pair of tall, blonde flight attendants went up to the pilots and after quick hugs all around, and sitting next to the pilots, moved into their private world.

Drug reps were more private. More competitive. She knew a few of them, but they were reluctant to trade secrets. Too much at stake. There were exceptions, of course, mostly among the more seasoned ones like herself. It seemed that the more knowledge they had, the firmer their hold on the industry, hence, they were less afraid of losing it.

Savannah knew that she was moving into that point in her career where she would have to start looking for different options. It was a daily struggle to keep up with, not only the constantly changing drug market, but also the technology alone required to make the presentations.

The young ones, coming out of college, came readily equipped with what she thought of as updated software. Just like her iPhone, Savannah had to constantly make updates to her brain. And it wasn't just technology and drugs. In order to establish rapport with the doctors younger than she was, she had to stay up with current culture. She had to know which movies were popular… which restaurants were popular in an area. Even what music people were listening to. And that didn't even begin to touch on what she had to keep up with in the political world. Who was supporting what movement. Such as the medical psychologists. Louisiana and New Mexico were allowing psychologists to write prescriptions. Several other states were right behind them. She had to be able to either support the idea or not depending on who she was interacting with.

All these things took their toll.

How dare Noah Worthington to waltz back nonchalantly into her life!

Hearing them call for first-class boarding, she gathered up her bag and was ushered through the gate. Following a couple down the corridor, she watched their heads tucked together, laughing at things unique to them, the rest of the world nonexistent.

A pang shot through her heart as they invoked unbidden, but now newly invoked memories of her year with Noah. They, too, had often walked hand in hand, oblivious to the rest of the world.

She followed them into the plane where they sat together and she sat across the aisle in her own private first-class seat. She always booked a single seat when possible. She enjoyed the privacy to read, work, or just rest her mind. Resting her mind often meant preparing herself for upcoming meetings.

She heard glimpses of the couple's conversation.

"Did you see the look on your father's face when his ex-wife asked him to dance?"

"I can't believe Meredith caught the bouquet. She's already thirty. Everyone knows she'll never get married."

Savannah smiled to herself. A happy couple on their honeymoon. This should be an interesting flight.

She accepted a bottle of water from the flight attendant and settled into her space. Flying at least once every couple of months, she was comfortable here. She had all the rules down. Drink lots of water. Stand up every hour. Avoid alcohol. Well, at least on the flight itself.

She took out a highlighter and a stack of notes. It was about time to unplug from the world for a few hours. But first, she sent a quick text to her mother. Another to her sister. Confirmed two appointments for next week. Set up a meeting with a new doctor she'd been assigned.

As the plane taxied down the runway, she turned off her phone and iPad. Sipped her water and relaxed a few minutes before getting to work.

She used the sway of the plane to prepare her mind to focus on reading.

The muted laughter of the couple next to her, snuggled in together now beneath a blanket provided by the flight attendant, faded into the background.

And Noah Worthington's face invaded her thoughts.

He looked better, she mused. He was nearing what Savannah considered a man's prime.

Handsome. Mature. Successful.

The very same profile of many of the men she dealt with on a daily basis. She had refined her interactions to an art. She knew how to get a man's attention and to keep it. She knew what to say to keep his focus in the midst of a busy day long enough to have him agree to use her medications.

She also knew when to let him down easily enough. Leaving him looking forward to their next meeting without feeling rejected.

In fact, she'd never dated a doctor. Or nurse. Or anyone in the health sciences.

Her five-year engagement had been to the construction manager who'd built her house on Lake Martin. She kept business and pleasure in two completely separate compartments.

Savannah Richards was good at her job. She knew her science. She knew her marketing techniques. She preferred solitude but was good at social interaction.

She hadn't however, been good enough at social interaction to keep the interest of Noah Worthington.

. . .

NOAH GATHERED UP HIS IPAD, tossed a tip on the table he had barely touched, and rushed out of the club. He had a flight to Dallas, then back in the morning.

Then his schedule was about to change. He had somewhere unexpected he needed to be.

He made his way down the concourse, into the terminal, and onto the plane. His copilot, a woman named Michelle, was running late from a delayed connection, so he had a few minutes to himself. To reflect on the conversation he'd had with his ghost from the past. He knew exactly when his divorce hearing was – December, but he hadn't wanted to talk about it with her.

Whether intentional or not, she'd presented him with a puzzle and Noah Worthington could not resist a challenge. Especially not one wrapped in such an appealing package.

She'd said she was going to be in New York for five days. That either meant she traveled so much that she would only be home for five days or she was travelling to New York. The thought of finding someone who lived in New York was daunting to say the least. But finding someone in a hotel narrowed it down slightly.

He began checking the weather. Skies were clear, so the routine check allowed him to think about Savannah Skye. He smiled at the name she obviously no longer used. He'd always thought how ironic and convenient, that both the girl he loved and the place he loved to be had the same name. Skye.

So she was a sales rep. What would a sales rep be doing in New York? Assuming she didn't live there, it was unlikely she would have clients there. "Ah ha," he said, picking up his iPad.

"Ah ha what?" Michelle asked, taking her seat next to him.

"You decided to show up for work?" he asked, pulling up google.

"You know how I am. Always trying to avoid a flight."

"Yep," Noah said. So, far, he'd found no gatherings of drug

reps in New York. Did drug reps even gather? Perhaps drug companies sponsor events. He googled drug companies and immediately found a list of twenty-five companies. This was going to take a while.

"So what's her name?"

"What?" Noah asked, after a few more clicks.

"Who is she?"

He stopped. Looked up blankly at his friend. Shook his head. "Who?"

"I haven't seen you this distracted since you had that crush on the brunette from Idaho."

Noah laughed and put his iPad aside to continue going through the pre-flight checklist with this copilot who had, over the years, become a friend of sorts. She was physically attractive, he supposed, but he'd never thought of her that way. She was tall, thin, and blonde; hence, she had a never-ending run of men. But it wasn't her looks so much that kept Noah at bay. It was the personality that doubtless came from the daily battle of trying to fit into a man's world.

"Back on match.com?" she asked.

"Nope."

"If you need a date, I can hook you up with a flight attendant."

"I'm good on my own. Thank you." He had made the mistake of allowing Michelle to *hook him up* once. One time too many. The match.com thing hadn't been for him either. He told himself that after seventeen years of marriage things had changed far too much in the dating world. It was a little more difficult to admit that he couldn't find anyone he could have a conversation with that he also wanted to kiss.

"Just say the word," Michelle said.

Noah preferred a woman who spoke like a lady. More times than not, Michelle's words could just as easily have come from a man.

"No crush," he said, needing to keep his thoughts about Savannah as far away from Michelle as possible. "Just information seeking."

"Ok," she said. "Looks like we should have an uneventful flight."

"The only way to fly," he said, automatically, truly not in the mood for pilot banter at the moment.

2

Noah sat in the cockpit of his plane, a Cessna Mustang with gray interior, running down the pre-flight checklist. He would be in New York by evening. It was already Thursday. That left only 4 days to not only track Savannah down, but also to convince her to spend time with him. He frankly didn't care if it was no more than a cup of coffee.

The plane was new – he'd only had it a few months, and only flown it three times, but he was already in love with it. He liked the idea of having his own space. No pilot banter. No crude jokes.

No forward flight attendants.

Noah supposed he was not the typical pilot. He loved flying. Passionately. He just didn't care for much of the culture that went along with it.

He taxied out to the runway and waited his turn. It would be a little while, but he didn't mind. He still had internet.

He'd run into a dead end with the twenty-five drug companies. Nothing seemed to be going on in New York that would attract a drug rep. Her words kept replaying in his head. *You know enough to find me.*

Had she been to New York before? That was a place she had always wanted to go. He recalled a cool fall Saturday they'd spent on Lake Martin on his boat. He winced at the memory that he'd told her it was a friend's.

There were so many things he hadn't told her.

The weather had been perfect. A soft breeze. The sun warm, but not hot. The leaves on shore starting to turn. The water calm. They were anchored in a quiet cove. Difficult to find this time of year. But Noah knew the lake inside and out. When he wasn't in the air, he had been in the water. His mother used to joke that he'd had something against land.

That's how it had been, anyway, before he met Savannah. After that, all bets were off. Even when he'd been in the air, he felt her pulling him back to her. Actually, now that he thought about it, he hadn't gone out in his boat again that year without taking her with him.

He'd brought a blanket and she had lain with her back against him, snuggled against his chest.

They had nothing to do that day. Mid-terms were over and they were taking a break. It was Saturday, so she wasn't at her student worker job.

"I can't think of anywhere I'd rather be," he'd said.

"Really? I can."

He hadn't answered right away.

"I'd want you with me," she added quickly.

He laughed. "I wasn't fishing. I was just trying to think of someplace better."

"Not necessarily better. Just different."

"I'm listening," he kissed the top of her head. He loved the way her hair smelled. He didn't tell her that, of course.

"San Francisco seems nice."

"California? That's like a whole different country out there. People are different."

She shifted, to glance at him. "How do you know?"

"I'm a pilot."

"Have you been there?"

"No. But I hear things."

"Ok. New York then."

He stroked her arm, instinctively holding onto her as a wave from a jet ski hit them. "Too big."

"That's what makes it so cool," she said. "So much history and so much energy. Right there in such a small space."

"Hmm."

"It's so big that most of it is in the sky."

He chuckled. "You like the idea of people living in the sky?"

"Yeah," she said. "Don't you? I mean of all people you should like it. You love riding in the sky, why not live in the sky?"

"That's an interesting concept, my love." He took her hand, held it in his. Marveled at how much smaller it was than his. How soft. "And very perceptive of you. I do love everything related to the sky." He waited a beat. "Savannah Skye."

"I have my moments."

"What would you do in New York in the sky?"

"I'd spend the day at the Empire State Building."

"It's not the tallest."

"Doesn't have to be. It's one of the oldest and has a wraparound view."

"They have a restaurant that turns while you eat."

"No way? How do you know that?" She shifted to glance at him before settling back against him.

"You have so little faith in how much I know."

He felt her laugh against him. "I don't think you know as much as you think you do."

"What would you do on the Empire State Building?"

"I'd look around at everything. I'd even look through those

telescopes they have. And…" she squeezed his hand. "I'd let you kiss me."

"Well," he said, pulling her around to face him, "Since you're taking me with you to your land in the sky, I suppose we'd better make sure we're in good practice."

She always smiled when he went to kiss her. It had bothered him at first, so much so that he'd once asked her about it.

"Why do you smile when I kiss you?"

She'd looked a little perplexed. "Because I like kissing you."

The voice on the radio indicated it was time for take-off. Pulling himself out his memories, he went to work. As he left the safety of land, his thoughts left the safety of the past.

Had she been to New York before? Had she been to the Empire State Building? Had she kissed someone there?

He should have been the one kissing her on the Empire State Building.

Landing in New York, he had to wait again. A line of planes all waiting their turn to get to a parking space. Opening his iPad, he went for a broad google search this time - *medication conferences.*

It took no more than a few keystrokes for him to feel the jolt of success.

There was a psychopharmacology conference going on right now.

In New York.

The American Society of Clinical Psychopharmacology.

She hadn't said she had a specialty.

It made sense though. He was only certified to fly certain types of airplanes.

It was being held at the Grand Hyatt Hotel.

He scrolled through the program.

And grinned like a cat who just stuck the claws of his paw into the tail of a mouse.

. . .

SAVANNAH SENT out for room service – a big salad with turkey and a bottle of water. She had read all the articles she had downloaded to read. And she already had a working draft that she'd started six months ago. She still had revisions to do on the PowerPoint before her presentation tomorrow morning. Her presentation was scheduled for 11:00 am. *The Drug Rep: An Inside View of the Unconscious.*

She'd done a similar presentation a couple of years ago, but this was a bigger – much bigger, conference and she wanted to make sure all her references were updated. And she had to make sure she had appropriate psychological jokes. Psychiatrists and psychologists wanted entertainment with their information.

Her plan was to give them just enough of a peek beneath the curtain, or as Sigmund Freud would say, a peek at the ankle – enough to keep them interested, but not enough to give anything away.

She looked at the notes scattered across the hotel desk and wondered how that had become the whole purpose of her life. Give them just enough – then get out.

It would be nice to just, once in a while, be able to let her guard down and say what she really wanted to say instead of what was expected. Or what would be most effective.

While she munched on a bite of egg, turkey, and spinach, someone knocked on the door. "Room service."

They must have made a mistake, she thought, walking across the room.

"I already have what I need," she said, through the door.

"We have a delivery for you," the man insisted.

Savannah didn't open the door. She trusted most of the strangers she came in contact with in her travels. However, the story of the drug rep brutally murdered in her hotel room in

Minneapolis had imprinted itself in her mind and she'd often considered how that could have happened. There were so many possibilities but Savannah always went for the most parsimonious.

"Just leave it," she said, "Thank you."

The man put something next to her door and walked off.

Savannah waited. She really couldn't be sure he'd left.

But if they'd brought her salad twice, she needed to call and straighten it out.

She walked back to her desk, drank some water, and walked back to the door. Waited. When she heard voices coming down the hall, she opened the door. If she was going to be nabbed, at least she'd have witnesses.

Instead of the food service tray she'd expected, there was a vase of red roses next to her door.

Two women walked down the hall, passed her, and no one else was visible.

She picked up the vase and took it into her room, locking the door behind her.

Keeping the flowers at arm's length, she took them to the bathroom and set them on the counter. Kept her eyes on them as though they would bite if she looked away. No one had sent her flowers since the construction worker and that had been at the beginning of their relationship.

Why would someone possibly send her flowers?

After several minutes had passed, with her mind frozen, she thought to look for a card and found one. The note was printed, so no handwriting to decipher.

Good luck with your presentation tomorrow.

She turned it over. There were no other identifying notes. Not even a florist name. That was odd.

Perhaps the conference coordinator had sent flowers out to all the presenters. That was the most logical explanation she could fathom.

If she, however, had been the conference coordinator, she would most definitely not send out the flowers of love to wish someone luck. White roses perhaps. Even better, would have been a bouquet of flowers with lilies, white roses, and white mini carnations in a blue vase. Maybe some white daisies. Definitely white flowers.

Instead, a vase of long-stem red roses with assorted fresh greenery and baby's breath in a silver vase sat on her bathroom counter.

Deciding they weren't going to do any damage, she took each bloom, one at a time, and examined it. They were perfectly formed rose buds. She sniffed. Definitely high quality. She counted them.

Frowned.

Counted three times more.

There were only eleven roses in the arrangement.

She shook her head, pushed them to the back of the counter against the mirror.

Unable to sort the whole thing out and make further sense of it, she double-checked the hotel room door lock, put it out of her mind, and went back to work on her presentation.

Around nine o'clock she realized her presentation was done. Sure, she could change up the font. Again. Or google some more images.

But as of right now, it was professional and comprehensive, but still entertaining.

She saved it on her computer. On the cloud. And emailed a copy to herself.

The next morning, she got up early, ran five miles on the treadmill in her room, and took a long hot shower after having eggs and fruit sent up for breakfast.

She put on a black pencil skirt with matching short jacket and an emerald camisole – to match her eyes.

She was focused and had her mind trained on her

presentation as she went down to the conference area at the hotel. In order to get into the social mode, she went into the vending area where the other sales reps would be.

"There you are," Adam, one of the reps from the Denver area pounced on her when she'd barely gotten in the door.

"Hey Adam. I see you made it." Adam was always at the conferences and he'd stayed in touch with Savannah throughout the years. They had drinks occasionally while at the conferences. They had, in fact, originally met in Chicago at a smaller conference.

"Wouldn't miss it," he said. "I've got to get back to my booth, but make sure you check out the STIM display back there."

"I thought you were anti-STIM."

"I am. They're gonna steal our business. Mark my words. But in the meantime, they have a cool display."

Savannah laughed. "I'll check it out."

Adam started to walk away, "Oh hey, drinks tonight?"

"Not tonight," she said. "We have that black-tie dinner thing."

"Right." He made a face. "Love those things."

"Just part of the job, Adam."

"Yep. Tomorrow night, then?" he asked, walking backwards.

"Sure," Savannah said absently. She never made casual commitments ahead of time at these things. Just in case she needed to be available for a business meeting. But she didn't really consider Adam a commitment. She was sure he felt the same way.

A little later, she stepped into a crowded meeting room. Everyone, it seemed wanted to know about the unconscious thoughts of a sales rep. *That's what I get for having a catchy title.*

Putting a smile on her face, she stepped into her extraverted role and began her presentation.

Everything went smoothly until a little over halfway

through. "So as you can see," she said. "from the next slide, the mechanism of action isn't all we worry about."

The next slide elicited a laugh. She had a cartoon up on the screen that had nothing to do with a drug's mechanism of action. It was Sigmund Freud himself, cigar in hand.

"However, back to busi." She froze in mid-sentence.

Her eyes fell on a man sitting in the second row on the left that she hadn't noticed before. He had been hidden behind a couple of what looked to be young physician assistants.

But this man was no doctor. She didn't need her knack for classifying people to figure this one out.

This man wore a smug grin that said *I found you sooner than you thought. And I just caught you terribly off guard.*

"Back to business," she continued, deftly putting Noah Worthington out her mind.

For a full two seconds.

After her presentation ended – exactly on time, several psychiatrists, two psychologists, and three other mental health workers came up, introduced themselves, and wanted to further the conversation.

She found the enthusiasm of the medical psychologists to be the most refreshing of all the medical professions she worked with. The medical psychologists used medications judiciously and effectively. They were apt to try other things in addition to medication. Savannah liked that about them and they responded well to her nonjudgmental response to their methods.

Psychiatrists, on the other hand, tended to see non-medication interventions as a waste of time. Depending on who they were speaking to, they may not come right out and say it, but medication was their only thing.

When the two psychologists asked to take her to lunch, she agreed, enjoying the twist of events. Usually, she was the one trying to take doctors to lunch to woo them into using her medications over another company's. But the psychologists seemed genuinely interested in establishing a relationship with her and learning more about the drug business.

She soon learned that they were from Louisiana. The woman, middle-aged, but looked Savannah's age, was a newly licensed medical psychologist. The man, in his early sixties, was her business partner. Though he was not a medical psychologist, he actually had more experience in the medical field than the newly licensed medical psychologist did. They seemed to work well together and enjoyed each other's company.

As they left the presentation room, Savannah scanned the room for Noah, but he had disappeared. She had the fleeting thought that she had imagined him. She had only glimpsed him the one time and then her view had been obstructed. The psychologists took her to the hotel café and they had a pleasant lunch. Savannah was honest with them. She didn't get to Louisiana often, but she could send an associate in the interim. She warned them that the associate would do her best to sway them to use their medications over those from other companies. They, however, seemed to expect this and weren't alarmed.

They ordered cocktails, so Savannah ordered a mimosa, her standby lunch drink. She found it difficult to keep her attention on them, even though she considered herself working. The thought that Noah was out there was disconcerting to say the least.

That despite insurmountable odds, he had managed to locate her in New York. She hadn't thought to ever see him again.

But there he had been, sitting in the audience of her presentation. The knowledge that he had found her sent little shivers through her. Little shivers that she thought had been eradicated from her system.

There was also the anticipation that she was destined to see him again. Although she could have doubtless found him after the presentation, she had needed to work. And… she had needed time to process the fact that he was, indeed here, in her hotel.

She finished her lunch and excused herself from the couple of psychologists. They had one more presentation they wanted to catch, then they were headed out to see the Statue of Liberty. She didn't blame them. If she didn't have obligations to be there, she would cut out, too. That was half the fun of going to conferences.

Not wanting to go back to her room just yet, she went to the courtyard and found a quiet place to respond to texts and emails. Her mother and sister had checked in. They had a bit of anxiety about her traveling alone though she'd been doing it her whole career. Her sister was a stay-at-home mom who devoted far too much time to worrying. And her mother was a retired school teacher, which pretty much summed things up in Savannah's mind. Her mother had pushed her relentlessly until she'd left home. Then Savannah had continued to push herself. Now her mother insisted that Savannah worked too hard.

MOTHER: *It's your, what, fourth or fifth time to New York? And you've never seen anything other than the inside of a hotel.*

SAVANNAH: *I happen to be sitting outside right now, Mom.*

MOTHER: *That doesn't count and you know it. Go see the Statue of Liberty, go to the Empire State Building, go shopping, for goodness sakes. You love shopping. And you're in the shopping mecca.*

Savannah sighed.

SAVANNAH: *I will, Mom. I go shopping every time I'm here. In fact, I might even go today.*

MOTHER: *Good. Just be careful out there.*

SAVANNAH: *Love you, Mom.*

There was a black-tie event tonight at the Art Institute.

Although she had brought something to wear, it wouldn't hurt to take a walk down 5th Avenue.

She gathered up her bags and went back inside the crowded hotel, making her way toward the elevators. She had the smile back on her face and greeted several acquaintances along the way.

She was looking forward to getting out of her heels and putting on some flats, at least until tonight.

As she reached the elevators and pressed the button, her smile faltered.

"Well, hello, Savannah Richards," Noah said, pushing himself off the wall to step toward her. "Are you staying here, too?"

Her heartbeat ratcheted up a notch. "You're stalking me now," she said.

He looked hurt. "I like to think of it more as… hunting."

She laughed. "Is that what they're calling it now?" She pressed the elevator button again.

"I'm always up for a challenge," he said.

"I wasn't challenging you, Noah. I was merely trying to… get away."

"It sounded like a challenge to me," he said, unable to hide the hurt on his face.

She sighed. "I'm actually rather impressed that you found me."

"It wasn't easy," he admitted. "Looks like you're having a busy day."

"Very."

"So, since I'm here. And you're here." He put his hands in his pockets and joined her in staring at the elevator. "Do you want to go have coffee?"

Coffee. With the man who broke her heart twenty years ago. That was exactly what she wanted to do. "I'm actually on my way out."

"Oh. I see," Again, that crestfallen look.

"But," she said, narrowing her eyes. "I have a black-tie affair tonight at the museum – a work thing. I was planning to go by myself, but I wouldn't mind having an escort." The offer of a black-tie affair usually sent most men running in the other direction.

"Black tie, huh? That happens to be my specialty."

She narrowed her eyes, looking for the joke. Didn't find it. "Great. I'll meet you in the lobby at 7:00."

Noah watched the doors of the elevator close and turned away. He'd been loitering around the elevators so long that the security guard had questioned him. Apparently waiting for someone at the elevator was a questionable excuse for standing around at this hotel.

He had a ridiculous grin on his face. She had been on target. He had felt like a stalker standing at the elevators for nearly two hours. His perseverance had paid off, though. In a hotel this large with this many people wandering around, it would have easy to lose track of her. It had been an anomaly that he'd seen her name in the presentation program. After her presentation, she'd been swamped with what he thought of as fans, then swept off to lunch with some people.

Although he wanted to talk to her, he wanted to do it in private. The last thing he wanted was to be an embarrassment to her.

But now… she had invited him to be with her in public. That meant he didn't embarrass her. She would have to introduce him. Spend hours with him.

There was just one problem.

He had to find a tux.

. . .

SAVANNAH SAT in the back of a taxi, locked in traffic. Tapping her foot. Tapping her fingers against her phone. She had taken far too long at the shops, but she had found the perfect dress for tonight. She didn't need shoes – wasn't into shoe fads. She liked basic pumps for all work and social occasions and wore flats on days like today. Of course, she also liked boots. Boots were sort of her weakness, but too big to travel with.

And added to that, she'd stopped in at one of the Blow Dry Bars to have her hair washed, blown and styled, then she had her make-up done and, finally, her nails. She'd chosen the mysterious look from a menu of make-up choices – smoky eyes, glossy lips. Her hair felt light, bouncy.

She checked the time on her phone. Again.

Took a deep breath.

She had plenty of time to get back to the hotel, change, and get back downstairs.

She should have just gotten dressed at the salon, she berated herself for the hundredth time. But her shoes were in her hotel room as well as her perfume.

I'll be fashionable late.

Nonetheless, with the magic of the New York minute, she arrived at the door to her hotel with forty-five minutes to get to her room, change, and make it back to the lobby.

Rushing into her room, she threw everything on the bed, plugged in her phone for a quick charge, and checked on the roses. They were still there and there were still only eleven of them.

With a little trill of girlish excitement, she unwrapped the black taffeta beaded gown with an off-the-shoulder bodice. The flower clustered sequins crowded the bodice and dispersed along the waist becoming scattered on the skirt. There was a royal blue sash at the waist, adding an elegant touch. The slit at the side was high – mid-thigh giving the formal column dress an unexpected edge.

She spritzed perfume high into the air, and walked through it. She adjusted the little diamond necklace she had bought herself last Christmas at Tiffany's and stepped into her shoes.

Checked the time. She had fifteen minutes to get downstairs. She grabbed her phone, tucked it into her handbag, and twirled in front of the mirror.

Black tie events are important to my career. Not everyone gets to go.

She ignored the other voice that reminded her that this one was different. She'd never taken a date.

It's not a date.

She'd never taken an escort.

It's Noah Worthington.

She laughed. Told herself to just enjoy the moment.

When she stepped into the lobby, she immediately realized she should have been more specific when she said to meet in the lobby.

Air and Water.

She found him near the waterfall, leaning against a column.

Her heart fluttered. She was again astounded that he was even more handsome than he was twenty years ago. Their clothing couldn't have matched more perfectly if they had tried. He wore a black tux with white shirt and royal blue tie. Six feet tall, broad shoulders, trim. A smile that would melt any female heart. He was clearly the most handsome man in the crowded lobby. A lobby the size of a basketball court.

She could tell he had watched her look for him. Felt the pink flush on her cheeks at his unwavering perusal.

He took a step forward, kept one hand in his pocket and one behind his back.

She returned his smile. Their gazes locked.

"You're beautiful," he said.

"You're not so bad yourself."

He took another step forward, brought a single long-stem red rose from behind his back. "To complete your set," he said.

She looked at the rose. Looked back at him. Back at the rose.

Oh. My.

It all clicked together for her. The eleven roses in her bathroom. The rose in his hand.

He held the rose out to her. She took it, her fingers trembling as she took it in her hands, avoiding the thorns. A white ribbon wound up the stem, and was tied into a bow.

She sniffed it, her eyes misting. Squeezing her eyes closed, she steadied herself.

Opened her eyes, her lips curving into a smile.

"Shall we make our way to the museum?" he asked, crooking his arm and holding it out to her.

She put her hand on his arm and followed him toward the front doors of the hotel. As they walked through the crowded lobby, people moved aside for them, but Savannah barely noticed them. She was ensconced in her own world.

With a handsome pilot. Off to a black-tie gala at the New York Metropolitan Museum of Art. Not bad for a girl from Birmingham, Alabama and a guy from Ft. Worth.

Outside the hotel, the doorman hustled to hail a cab.

"Wait here for a second," he whispered in Savannah's ear.

He stepped up to the valet stand, spoke to the valet, and came back to her side. "Our car will be here in five minutes," he said, waving off the taxi.

"We're not taking a taxi?"

"Not tonight," he said.

It was more than five minutes, but less than ten, when a sleek, black limo pulled up to the curb. The valet appeared at the car, opened it, and ushered them forward.

Settled into the back of the limo, he smiled.

"Nice touch," she said.

"Can't be riding around in a taxi dressed like this," he said.

"I'm a little impressed," she said.

"Then it was worth it."

"I'm not easily impressed," she said.

"I didn't think you were. So, who are we meeting with tonight?"

"It's hosted by one of the top five drug companies."

"Big pharma."

"None other."

"Is this the one you work for then?"

"It's crazy, but no. You might say I'm one of the competitor representatives."

"That sounds like quite an honor."

"It's actually more like an obligation."

Noah pulled a bottle of champagne from the ice bucket in front of them and filled two flutes. Handed one to her. "Here's to obligations," he said, touching his glass to hers.

"To obligations," she said and sipping. This was a Noah that she didn't know; nor had she expected.

The Noah that she had known was a devil-may-care daredevil. He drove a black Mustang and wore white t-shirts. Though she knew him to be disciplined and hard-working, her memory had created an image of him as something of a bad boy.

Noah had never given her flowers, nor had he ever taken her to a gala in a limo. While wearing a tuxedo. And he had certainly never given her champagne.

They had drunk beer on his boat on Lake Martin, wearing swimsuits, and shorts.

"Penny for your thoughts," he said.

"I was remembering beer on Lake Martin. Wondering how we'd ended up drinking champagne in New York in what feels like the blink of an eye."

"Life is full of surprises, isn't it?" he asked.

"How did you find me?"

"You told me you'd be in New York."

"How did you know I didn't live here?

"I was betting on the come."

"There you go with gambling references again."

"It means I'm betting on the future."

"I know what it means," she said, sipping bubbles from her glass. "I'm not sure what it means in this case."

"It means if you lived here, I never would have found you. But if you were visiting, you had to be staying at one of the hotels. And you were obviously here for some kind of business thing. From there, I looked for drug conferences."

"It's not really a drug conference."

"Not exactly, no, which made it a bit more difficult."

Before they could finish their conversation, they pulled up in front of the Met and the driver opened their door.

Replacing the typical tourist crowd from daytime, the Met was overflowing with ladies dressed in formal evening gowns and men in tuxes. These were the business moguls of the drug companies, physicians, and representatives like Savannah.

And their dates.

Or escorts.

It was all semantics, Savannah mused as she walked up the steps with her hand on Noah's arm. They could be perfect strangers, having met in the cab, but once they appeared together at the gala, they were automatically thought to be a couple.

Adam was the first person she recognized. He must have been watching for her. She ignored the little pang of guilt at not warning him that this time, unlike years before, she wouldn't be sitting with him.

"Adam," she said, "this is Noah."

Noah and Adam shook hands, seemed to size each other up.

"Savannah didn't mention she was bringing a date," Adam said.

"I don't think she knew until today," Noah said.

"I see," Adam said.

"Noah and I were friends in college," Savannah stated.

"I see," Adam said, seeming to bristle a bit. "Are you a doctor?"

"No, I'm a pilot."

"Oh," Adam said, then was silent.

"Well," Savannah said. "We should go inside. It's about time for them to get started."

"Of course," Adam said, stepping aside.

Savannah and Noah went through the museum to the room set aside for tonight's occasion. There were several small groups clustered around the room.

"We should really spend some time in here," Noah said, as they passed several paintings.

Savannah glanced at him askance. "Really? You like art?"

"Yeah," he said. "Who doesn't?"

She shrugged and took a glass of champagne from a passing server. "Not a lot of free time," she murmured.

He shifted. Faced her. "Are you telling me your life is all work and no play?"

She studied the bubbles in her glass. "I work a lot."

"How long has it been?"

As her thoughts went places she typically didn't think so much about, she felt her face flush. "How long?" she echoed thickly.

He beamed. "Since you had a date."

She laughed.

"But we can talk about… the other if you want to."

"Four years," she said. "Four years since I had a boyfriend. And I haven't dated really since then."

"Haven't dated much or at all?"

"You're awfully inquisitive," she turned her gaze to an abstract painting – splashes of black and white that resembled the work of a three-year-old.

"I want to know everything," he said.

This time, she flushed in earnest. "My life is rather boring."

He scoffed. "Your life has never come close to being boring."

She bit her lip. A flurry of possible responses ran through her head. Before she could land on one of them, they were interrupted by Mr. Pence, CEO of one of the big drug companies hosting tonight's gala.

"Miss Savannah Richards," he greeted her with obvious enthusiasm, taking her hand. "I'm so glad you could make it tonight."

"I wouldn't miss it for the world. Mr. Pence, I'd like you to meet my friend, Noah Worthington," she said as she pulled her hand from his.

"It's a pleasure to meet you. Are you a physician?"

"No, I'm not a doctor, I'm a pilot."

"Oh," Mr. Pence said, a similar expression to the one Adam had worn upon hearing the news that Savannah had brought an outsider into their folds. "Well, then, this should be interesting to you."

"It is interesting to see the inside of Savannah's world."

"She's had a successful career," Mr. Pence said.

"Hopefully you're not putting me out to pasture yet," Savannah said, with a laugh.

"Absolutely not," the older man said. "In fact, I should warn you Mr. Worthington that if you have designs on Savannah, we won't let her go without a fight."

"I wouldn't think of taking her away from the thing she loves."

"Good. Good," Mr. Pence said. "Well, enjoy yourselves. There's food in the next room."

After he walked out of earshot, Savannah rolled her eyes. "Designs on me?"

"I think it shows great affection on his part to be worried about you."

"Designs?"

"It's cute," he said. "Remember, he's from a different generation."

"Oh, I get that. But he made an awful lot of assumptions by you standing next to me."

"You did introduce me as your friend," he reminded her, "Come on, I'm starved."

When they stood in front of the food display, he pinned his gaze to hers. "Just say the word. I'll have you out of here and in a fancy restaurant."

She shook her head and led him toward the other room. "As tempting as that sounds, I don't think it's a good idea. They would put me out to pasture for sure."

He handed her a plate, stepped aside for her to go first. She put some cheese, a raspberry crepe, and some crab salad on her plate. He followed suit.

"I can get us in to a nice restaurant," he said as they sat at an empty table, covered with a white tablecloth.

"This is just the appetizer," she said.

He chuckled. "If you insist."

Another of Savannah's colleagues came up and hugged Savannah. She looked at Noah with a big smile.

"I'm a pilot," he said, before she could ask.

"Oh. Wow," the young woman said, glancing at Savannah.

"We're friends," Savannah said.

"Oh. Ok. I thought..."

Noah laughed.

"We'll talk later, Savannah," the woman said and moved away.

"She thought I brought my pilot to dinner," Savannah said, under her breath.

"Actually," Noah said, biting into a crepe. "It's customary."

"Customary?"

"It's not unusual for people to bring their private pilots with them to things like this."

Savannah tucked her hair behind her ears. "You work for the airline."

"I do," he said. "But they don't know that."

Savannah looked around the room. Many of the guests were wealthy, powerful people. She was a drug representative. Not really part of this world. Not on a day to day basis. Only during special events like this.

"They think I hired a private pilot."

"That would be my guess," Noah said, keeping his focus on her. "So, you can expect that they'll look at you a little differently from now on. Unless, of course, you set them straight."

Her lips curved into a mysterious smile. "I don't know why I would do that. I rather like the idea of having my own private pilot."

"That opens all sorts of doors in my head."

She rolled her eyes at him, but secretly enjoyed that he still had those doors he was willing to open for her.

"Have you thought about doing that?" she asked.

His eyes widened and she had to quickly swallow her water to avoid spewing. "Let me rephrase that. Have you thought about hiring out as a private pilot?"

"I have thought about that," he said.

"Well, have you ever done it?"

"Yes," he said, but she could see the shutters close in his face. And she was not surprised when he changed the subject. "What do you want to do after this?" he asked.

"After the conference?"

"After the gala."

"It'll be late," she said.

"You have an early morning?"

"Only if I want to. With my presentation over, I don't really have any obligations."

"Yet you're staying until Tuesday."

"Yeah, I'll probably catch some workshops."

"Savannah," he said. "You do know the real reason people go to conferences."

"To learn," she insisted.

He rolled his eyes.

"And to network."

"Those are good reasons. They also go to get away. To have fun."

"I am having fun," she said.

He smiled. "That's good to know. Then perhaps you'd like to have some non-conference fun. Unless of course, you can't handle it."

"Of course, I can handle it."

"Name one thing in New York that you've always wanted to do, but haven't done."

"Easy. I'd like to go up the Empire State Building."

"And… you've never done that."

She shook her head.

"You do realize that's the first thing people do when they come to New York."

She shrugged. "I've never done it."

"You've never been to the Statue of Liberty."

She shook her head. "But…" she held up her hand. "I've been shopping on Fifth Avenue. In fact, I was there today."

"That's a relief. I was beginning to worry about you."

"Now you're making fun."

"Nope. Now I know what I can do for you."

"Ha."

He grinned. "One of many things."

The speaker, Mr. Pence, came on the microphone, and Savannah realized the room had filled and people were seated all around them.

Mr. Pence began talking as dinner was served. Savannah quickly regretted her decision to not duck out and go to that fancy restaurant Noah had offered. The food was bland and the speech predictable.

She leaned over, put her lips next to Noah's ear. "Do you still want to get out of here?"

"Just say the word," he said, turning, his face near hers. His lips a hair's breadth from hers.

Her heart stuttered as her gaze landed on his lips. Although she had kissed those lips hundreds of times before, it was as though she never had.

He was a different man now with twenty years between. Twenty unknown years. The disconnect was intriguing.

What would it feel like to kiss him? Would it be familiar or would it be brand new? She swallowed thickly. She lifted her gaze back to his and she was lost in those pools of blue.

Noah Worthington was an intriguing man. There was so much she knew. So much she didn't know.

And, oh so very much that she wanted to know.

GETTING her out was proving to be more difficult than he had expected. Savannah, unfortunately, was obligated to be here for work. If she boldly got up and walked out, she would be noticed. And judged. Noah could do black tie events in his sleep. Especially one where no one knew him and he was free to sit in the background and observe.

That didn't mean that he wanted to be here.

He wanted to be with Savannah, but preferably alone with her.

As Pence was wrapping up his speech, Noah took the opportunity to set their exit in motion. "When I say go, meet me out in front of the restrooms," he said.

She nodded. Waited until the applause started.

"Now," he said. And was pleasantly surprised when she got up and made her way out of the room.

He waited a couple of minutes. Then followed her out.

She smiled sheepishly as they dashed out the front door of the museum. She waited while he had the limo brought around. Her cheeks were flushed a bit with excitement. He couldn't help staring at her. She was glowing.

And he was spellbound.

And honored that he had been the one to talk her into doing the thing that put that flush on her face.

He didn't want to let her down.

Ever.

Again.

"Where are we going?" she asked, as the car pulled out into the traffic.

"It's a surprise," he said.

"I don't like surprises."

"I know. But you'll like this one."

She grinned at him, shook her head. "You haven't changed one single bit."

"And you've developed a mean streak," he said with a feigned look of hurt.

She chuckled. "You have no idea."

"You have my attention now," he said.

"I'll keep that in mind."

They rode in silence for a few minutes. He soaked in every angle of her face, every movement of her lips. Even in twenty years, she was perfect – better even than before and he couldn't take his eyes off her.

"You're staring," she said.

"You're pretty," he said.

She chuckled again, her face flushing. "You're being silly."

"It's like that first day all over again."

She stared back him then, her lips curving into that sexy little confident smile that he loved. "It is, isn't it?"

The car stopped and he helped her out, taking her hand. He didn't let go as they went into the doors of the Empire State Building.

"Aren't they closed?" She asked.

He led her to the ticket counter, bought two tickets and went to the elevators where there was a line. "They're open," he said. "And the best time to visit is at night."

"Hmm," she said.

They got into the elevator and started up. He watched the play of emotions on her face. The emotions she hid well. There was a bit of trepidation as the elevator creaked and started up, mixed with a bit of excitement.

When they got out at the top, they went to the outside door and, stepping outside into the wind and darkness, high above the streets of New York, she gasped. "Wow."

"Yeah," he said, keeping a firm hold on her hand as they stepped out to the railing.

"This is so beautiful." She whispered.

"Come around here. Look at Central Park."

They walked around, gazing at the busy life of New York far below them. The cool breeze picked up on the other side. She shivered.

He took off his jacket and placed it around her shoulders. With a look of gratitude, she slipped her arms in the sleeves and disappeared into his jacket that was much too big for her.

"Wouldn't it be awesome to live here? So much energy," she said.

"A far cry from the small town of Birmingham or Auburn."

"There isn't even a comparison."

"Where do you live now?" he asked.

"Lake Martin," she said.

She answered easily, not realizing the effect her words would have on him. They had spent countless hours there on the lake. The fact that she had chosen to make her home there, almost caused him to come undone.

"You remember it, right?" she asked, focused on the city.

"Yes," he said, his voice hoarse. He cleared his throat.

She turned, looked at him. Studied his face. "You're surprised," she said.

Noah felt a lump in his throat that threatened to send tears to his eyes. After all he put her through, she was able to stay there, where they had been connected, and make her life.

"Noah," she whispered, placing a hand on his cheek.

He sucked in his breath, determined not to allow his thoughts – his regrets to overcome him now.

He put his hand over hers, smiled, wobbly as it felt, and squeezed as he enveloped both her hands in his. They were mere inches apart. He moved forward, kissed her on the forehead.

Her eyes fluttered closed. He gently turned her, pulled her against him, and rested her back against his chest. His chin fit perfectly on the top of her head.

Just as he remembered.

Together, they watched the traffic below, the lights of the city all around them. Others, mostly couples, walked around them, leaving them alone in their own little world.

He could feel her heartbeat against his chest. Or maybe he imagined it. Maybe it was his own heart beating. He could feel her warm breath against his hand as his arms were wrapped around her. She hesitated, but rested her arms against his.

Noah could not have been more content in that moment.

He was in a beautiful place with the most beautiful girl in

the world. There was no one else he could possibly want to be with.

He didn't know how long they stood there, neither one wanting to move.

He heard a clock strike midnight and she tensed against him.

"We should go," she said.

He wasn't sure if it was a question or a statement. "Are you going to turn into a pumpkin?"

"Cinderella didn't turn into a pumpkin, the carriage did."

"But something about the stroke of midnight..."

"Makes it feel like it's all going to end."

"It doesn't have to end. She could have stayed with the prince instead of running off." Noah had never understood that.

"She couldn't let him find out who she really was."

"It wouldn't have mattered. He was already in love with her."

"He only met her hours before."

"It happens."

"But she couldn't have known that."

"She needed to have faith."

"Then there wouldn't have been a story."

"There was a story alright."

She sighed. "A big part of the story was that he had to search for her."

"It didn't have to be that way, but you're probably right," he admitted. "Men often don't

realize what they have until it's gone."

"You know this from experience?"

"No," he said. "You're right. We should probably go."

He led her back to the elevators, and silent now, they traveled down. She kept her hands hidden in his jacket. He stared at the numbers as the dial ticked downward.

He wanted to tell her everything. He wanted to explain. He wanted her to understand.

But not now.

He wasn't ready to break the spell.

He wasn't ready to risk her rejecting him for what he had done.

He told himself that the damage had been done twenty years ago. If he told her the truth, would it only make things worse? He just wanted it all to be behind them.

He wanted to begin again.

SAVANNAH KNEW the moment Noah retreated into himself. She kicked herself all the way down the elevator.

It was too soon to bring up the past.

They were just at the beginning of starting over. It would do no good to bring it all up again anyway.

They had to let it go if they were going to start over.

She just had so many questions. So many unanswered questions.

They couldn't deny the unfinished business. It was part of who they were.

But she would give it time.

She would give it time because she liked who he was. Liked who they were together.

They got back to the hotel and went through the lobby, nearly deserted now.

At the elevators, she took his hand. Smiled at him. "Thank you for coming with me tonight."

He brought her hand to his lips, kissed her palm. "Have breakfast with me," he said.

She knew better than to try and understand his changing moods. "I plan to sleep through breakfast," she said. "Remember, I turn into a pumpkin at Midnight."

He chuckled and pulled her against him in a hug. "Lunch then?" he asked, holding her elbows.

"Alright. I'll have lunch with you."

The elevator door opened and they went inside. "Keep the rest of the day open, too. I have a surprise for you."

"I don't like surprises."

"I know, but you'll love this one."

They got off at her floor. She handed him the rose she had remembered to pick up from the seat in the limo and pulled her phone out of her handbag. "I'm here," she said, when they got to her door. She held her phone to her door and it unlocked. He reached behind her, opened the door and stepped aside for her.

"Good night," he said, handing the rose back to her.

"Good night," she said, walking through the door, letting him close it behind her.

She stood staring at the closed door. Let the range of emotions wash over her.

This was a day she had never, ever expected. After twenty years.

In the span of mere days, she had accidentally run into her college sweetheart, set an impossible path for him to find her a second time in New York, and spent a fairytale evening with him.

She stepped out of her shoes and walked into the bathroom with her rose. She pulled the vase forward and slid the rose into the vase. Twelve roses now.

She smiled to herself at the romantic gesture.

She took the roses into the bedroom and placed them on the dresser. She sat on the edge of the bed and realized she still wore his jacket.

Taking it off, she pressed her face against it. And inhaled deeply.

She missed him.

How could she miss him already?

This was not a good sign.

He had told her two days ago that he wasn't even divorced yet.

She groaned.

She wasn't sure what it said about her, but she didn't care. She wanted to spend time with him. She wanted to know the answers.

Twenty years ago he had gone back to visit his parents. He had called it a summons. He had evaded telling her much other than it was a business meeting with someone his father had known since childhood.

Three weeks later, he had graduated, packed up and gone back to Ft. Worth.

They hadn't broken up. He'd said he'd call. That was before they had cell phones.

He hadn't called.

She'd never even known if he made it home. She'd gone to the Internet to try and find news of an accident.

All she knew was that he lived with his parents in Ft. Worth. She knew their names were Martin and Mary Worthington. She had looked, but she hadn't been able to locate them online.

She'd gone about her summer – school and student worker job.

But she had grieved.

And buried herself in her studies.

She'd looked for him a few times over the years, but unsuccessfully. As far as she had been concerned, he had fallen off the face of the earth.

She wanted to know the answers.

Because she had never stopped loving him.

. . .

Savannah was up at seven the next morning. She jumped on the treadmill, and ordered room service – yogurt and granola today. She flipped through the conference program and found a couple of presentations that she had highlighted to possibly attend.

Instead, she indulged herself and ran a hot bubble bath. She replayed last night over and over in her head.

Found herself looking forward to the day. With Noah. Whatever it may hold.

She put on some jeans and a casual shirt, pulled her hair back, put on a pair of dark sunshades, and slipped out to the elevators.

After stopping by Starbucks for a grande vanilla latte with caramel drizzle, she went to the blow out bar around the corner. She had her hair washed and dried and her make-up done in what they called natural.

With it being Saturday morning, the blow out bar was packed. Whoever came up with the idea was an absolute genius and her credit card was fortunate that this New York indulgence hadn't caught on in Birmingham. Sure, she could go to a salon, but that was typically for a haircut, too, and they didn't do make-up.

After her morning of being pampered, she went back to the hotel and changed clothes three times. She decided against blue jeans and quickly ruled out a skirt and jacket.

She put on the red dress she'd originally brought for last night's gala, added a little cardigan, put on the chunky red lace-up heels she had bought to match, and studied herself in the mirror.

The dress was red jacquard flower print, with a high low hem – just above her knees in the front and halfway down her calves in the back. The sales lady had said it could be dressed up or down. Since she had no idea what Noah had planned for the day, she thought she could pass for whatever he came up with. She could always remove the cardigan for a dressier look for dinner.

She checked the clock and paced a bit. He hadn't said what time he would be there to pick her up or even where they would meet.

It was ten to noon. She sniffed the roses, and fought back the panic that he wouldn't show up.

What if he just didn't? She had no way to contact him.

He won't disappear again.

He had acted a little distant after she'd brought up the past, but then he'd asked her to spend the day with him.

If he stands me up, I won't see him again.

Going to the window, she took deep, steading breaths.

I shouldn't have gone to so much trouble getting ready.

Feeling a little foolish, she located the remote and checked the weather. It was going to be a beautiful day.

If he's not here by one o'clock, I'm going to walk around the city myself. She'd seen an interesting little restaurant around the corner that looked like a good lunch spot.

When he knocked on the door, she jumped and fumbled the remote.

She went to the door, confirmed that it was him, and opened the door.

"Hi," he said, "you look a little startled."

"Do I?" She turned her anxiety into a bright smile.

"Yes, you do, but nonetheless stunning."

"You look good," she said. He was wearing khaki pants with loafers and a pale pink shirt, open at the collar. He wore a leather case hanging from a strap across his shoulders.

"I'm overdressed," she said, biting her lip.

"You're perfect," he said. "Ready for lunch?"

"Starved."

They fell into any easy rhythm going downstairs, out onto the street.

He glanced at her shoes, "I'll get a taxi."

Once inside the back seat, he gave the driver an address.

"What's for lunch?"

He winked at her.

"I know," she said. "It's a surprise."

He laughed. "You always were a quick study."

"Yeah," *And I've always been a sucker for you.*

They only went three blocks before the driver pulled up to the curb and they got out. Taking her hand, Noah led her to the door of a quintessential pizza parlor.

"Pizza," she said, letting her guard down.

"This may be your third time to New York, but this time you get to really experience it."

He was staring at her again, but she didn't care. There was a line out the door, but she didn't care.

He was right. She'd never had New York pizza.

As they stood in line, he asked. "Exactly what have you done during your time in New York?"

"Let see... I've ridden the subway. I've been to the Met obviously. And I've been shopping on Fifth Avenue. Oh. And I discovered blow out bars."

He gave her an odd look. "Blow out bar?"

She laughed. Swirled her hair.

"Ah. Haircut."

"Not a cut. Just a blow dry."

He ran a hand through her hair. "Nice," he said. "Ok, so shopping, art museum, and hair."

"And subway."

"Right. And art isn't really your thing."

"I don't dislike it."

"There's a big difference between liking something and disliking it." He unzipped his case and pulled out his iPad.

"Ah," she said.

"Ah what?"

"Ah, I wondered what you had in there."

"A pilot is never without his iPad."

"Really? We use iPads, too, for medications."

"Then you understand."

"Yeah, but I'm not working right now."

"A pilot is always on call."

"Always?"

"Pretty much. Yeah."

He made a few clicks on his iPad. "Done," he said.

"Work?"

"Not this time," he said with a wink.

"Personal?"

"Part of your surprise."

NOAH HAD to make some last-minute adjustments in his plan. The weather had been perfect for the Staten Island Ferry and the Statue of Liberty. But Savannah had come out wearing something looking more like an evening dress and heels than for walking around as a tourist. He would ask her to wear jeans and flats tomorrow. But not yet. She had obviously put a lot of detail into today's attire.

And he was enjoying it far too much to ruin it for her.

After cheese pizza, they hopped back in a taxi and went to Broadway.

She didn't even ask where they were going.

Instead, she wore a look of eager anticipation. He considered that a huge step for someone who didn't like surprises.

The taxi dropped them at the door to the Phantom of the Opera house. Her eyes widened. "Really?"

"We have tickets for the two o'clock showing."

She beamed.

"Since you don't like surprises," he said. "I'll go ahead and tell you the plan so you know what to expect. After this, we'll have drinks at the Rainbow Room followed by dinner."

That part of his plan, at least, they could keep.

She put her arm on his, leaned in, and kissed him on the cheek. "Thank you."

Once they had made their way to their seats, he took her hand. "I'm sorry," he said. "about last night."

"What do you have to be sorry about?"

"You asked me a question I wasn't ready to answer. I didn't want to ruin the mood. But I owe it to you to answer questions you might have. And I will. I'll tell you what happened tonight."

"I should be the one apologizing. You obviously weren't ready to talk about it. Whatever it was that happened, I'm sure you had a good reason. Anyway, I don't want to ruin the mood either."

"Sounds like we're on the same page. When you're ready to know, I'm ready to tell you."

"That means a lot."

Noah preferred a good movie with a storyline he could understand to singing he couldn't. But halfway through, Savannah was moved to tears. He had to admit that the special effects were quite impressive.

"What do you think?" she asked at intermission.

"I don't dislike it," he said.

She laughed.

"If you want to stretch your legs, I'll buy us a drink,"

A few minutes later, they returned to their seats with glasses of red wine.

"This should make it much better," he said.

She shook her head. "Only spoken by the guy from Ft. Worth."

"What can I say? We had rodeos, not operas."

After the play, they went to the Rainbow Room for drinks

as he had promised. Savannah ordered a cosmopolitan – with olives and he ordered a crown on the rocks.

"You look beautiful tonight," he said.

"I never once imagined us here."

"I knew our paths would cross again."

That elicited that look again. The one that said perhaps he should be on an antipsychotic medication.

"Why would you think that?"

"Because I would have looked you up. And you have to admit I'm a pretty good detective."

"You did find me in New York. And I am impressed by that. But I gave you enough clues. Do you know how hard it is to find someone without clues?"

"You could have found me."

"Really? Tell me how."

"You knew I was from Ft. Worth. You knew my parents' names – unless you forgot, which is quite natural. And you knew I was a pilot."

"Actually, that wasn't enough."

"No?"

"No. I looked for you."

"It's ok," he said. "It wasn't your job to find me. It was my job to find you."

"Anyway," she said, tipping the lime into her glass and sliding an olive off the toothpick into her mouth. "I've always had a gut feeling that it had something to do with the summons from your father that weekend."

"The summons."

"Am I right?"

"You are exactly right."

"What was it about?"

He stirred his drink.

"You said you'd answer. But if you don't it's ok."

3

NOAH — BEFORE

Noah didn't want to be here. A summons from his father, Martin Worthington, was never a good sign. And this was two in less than thirty days.

He tied his shoes and smoothed out his tux. *Just get it over with.*

He walked down to the drawing room where his father was already entertaining. His father had promised that there would be only a few guests.

A few guests to his father could be five or a hundred.

Noah saw his mother, fussing with a flower arrangement, her blonde hair in a simple updo. She was elegant in a dark blue sheath dress.

"Noah," she said, hugging him. His mother hadn't come from money. She'd been a self-employed florist until his father had swept into her life and given her a fairytale romance – at least for a while.

Noah knew he wasn't supposed to be an only child. But he had been. His mother wouldn't talk about it. Whenever the topic came up, his mother had a haunted look in her eyes and his father turned away, with silence.

Always silence when he was displeased.

Growing up, Noah had loved it when his father was away on business. Without his father there, he and his mother would veg out on pizza and watch movies. Sometimes she would even play video games with him. Of course, when he'd hit teenage years, he chosen to do things with his friends.

Nonetheless, his mother was the one he could talk to.

"What's Dad up to?" he asked.

His mother kept her eyes on the flowers. "Just his usual," she said. "Everything is a business deal."

"I can't imagine why that would require a summons for me."

He expected his mother's usual *It's not a summons, Dear, he just wants to see you.* Instead, she said, "He's getting older. I think he's trying to get everything in order."

Noah glanced at his father, his head bent in deep conversation with another man, a little older than he. "Dad? Older? He'd never admit to that."

"Whether he admits to it or not, it's inevitable for all of us."

Before he could question his mother further, his father had spotted him and called him over. "Noah, get over here. This is Mr. Henry Beauchamp. We've been friends since we were in high school."

"Really?" Noah shook the older man's hand. "I'm surprised we haven't met."

"Mr. Beauchamp moved to California shortly after high school and we lost touch for a few years."

"Have you moved back, then?" Noah asked.

"Oh no. Just expanding a business venture back this way."

"Oh, well, Dad is the one to meet with on that."

His father had laughed, but even to Noah, it had sounded a little nervous.

"My wife will be here shortly," Henry said. "It was good of you to have us for dinner."

"You're welcome here anytime," his father said.

"Your father tells me you're a pilot," Henry said.

"I am," Noah said. "I'll have my degree by the end of the month and I have several job options available."

The two older men exchanged looks.

Noah no longer questioned his father. The two of them weren't close. Martin made sure Noah remembered that he was the son and Martin was the father.

"That should make you invaluable to the family business," Henry commented.

"Why don't you make yourself a drink, Noah?" his father suggested.

"I apologize," Henry said, "I would never keep a man from his evening cocktail."

Noah obediently left the men and went to the well-stocked bar across the room. He dismissed the men's conversation. His father's business, really, was no concern of his. He was a pilot and would soon be flying for the one of the larger airlines.

This party, it seemed, was going to be smaller than his father's usual. Noah was still perplexed about why his father had asked him to come tonight. He hadn't overly questioned it, however, because it had given him an opportunity to fly. And any opportunity to fly was always welcome in his book.

Noah poured scotch into a glass. Added ice. Wondered what Savannah was doing. Checked his watch and thought about calling her. He looked around for his mother, but she had disappeared.

Noah took his glass and went out on the veranda. There was a cool breeze at the moment. Summer had yet to take full root. But it wouldn't be long before the summer heat was unbearable.

He had wanted to bring Savannah. He wanted to bring her everywhere. In fact, he would have brought her, but something in his father's voice had alarmed him. That alarm coupled with

Savannah's pending final exams had kept him from pushing at her to come along.

It was just as well, he thought. Savannah knew him as the laid-back college student majoring in aviation who had an occasional beer.

She would not know him as this man who wore a tux to an everyday business dinner meeting with his family and drank scotch from what she would call fancy crystal glasses. And had dinner in a dining room twice the size of her whole dorm common room.

Female voices caught his attention and he turned his thoughts back to the present. Whatever it was his father wanted, he was waiting until morning to discuss it with Noah. *I could have flown in tomorrow morning and missed all this.* For some reason, his father seemed to enjoy torturing him whenever he had the opportunity.

Hearing his father call his name, he went back inside and stood watching for a moment.

Two women had entered the room. One appeared to be Henry's wife – a brunette with shoulder-length hair, but it was the other that sent the hairs standing up along his nape.

She was a tall blonde, with long, straight hair, a pretty smile. She was young – about Noah's age and wore a seductive red dress with matching red heels. Even her lips, curved into a bow, were red.

Noah's first impression was *trouble.*

"Noah," his father insisted. "Come meet Claire."

Noah stepped forward. Claire held out her hand, but with her palm down. It was the way women of wealth shook hands with men. Noah imagined that older men actually would kiss the lady's hand.

Savannah would have laughed. And said that Claire would never make it in the business world. What she wouldn't have understood was that Claire would never have to make it in the traditional business world. This was her world. And this was how she would make it.

"I've heard so much about you" Claire said.

"And I've heard absolutely nothing about you," Noah admitted, after a brief touch of the girl's hand.

"It seems our fathers have known each other our whole lives."

Noah began to get a sick feeling in the pit of his stomach.

"There's plenty of time to get acquainted," Noah's mother, who had reappeared stated. "Dinner is ready. Shall we?"

They went into the dining room. Noah was surprised that the dinner party only included six people. The alarm bells in his head were at full decibel as he was seated next to Claire at the table.

Nonetheless, the dinner conversation was pleasant enough. Claire and her mother talked about their flight from California and their day of shopping in Ft. Worth.

Apparently, they found great humor in Texas styles. Nonetheless, they had each bought themselves a Texas cowboy hat as a souvenir.

"Where in California do you live?" Noah asked.

"Los Angeles," Claire answered. "I can't imagine living anywhere else. The climate is great and the food is good especially for me, being a vegan. I had trouble finding anything I could eat today."

"Everything has beef in it," Claire's mother added.

"Image that," Noah said. Checking his watch under the table. He needed to call Savannah, but didn't want to call too late. She liked to go to sleep early, but had promised to wait up until after he called. "I guess that explains the salad and vegetables."

"I guess it does," Claire answered, her smile curved into a knowing bow.

After a few more minutes of inane conversation, Noah

excused himself. "I have to make a call to someone back east," he said, pushing his chair away from the table. "Please excuse me."

He truly couldn't get away fast enough. His father was obviously trying to push through a new deal, but he would have to do it on his own. He'd done it enough times before.

"Hi love," he said when Savannah answered.

"Hey," she answered sleepily.

"I'm sorry it's so late."

"It's not late. Studying makes me sleepy."

"I know."

"Did you find out what your father wanted?"

"No," Noah said, "He had some guy over for a business meeting. I'm sure he'll let me know tomorrow what he needed me for."

"Maybe he just wanted to show off his son."

"Not likely. That isn't his style."

"How's your mother?" she asked.

"A little reserved," he said.

"Hmm."

"It seems a little odd, doesn't it?"

"I don't really know them all that well, but, well… yes."

Noah smiled. That was one thing he loved about Savannah. She didn't mind saying what she thought. Coupled with her high level of perceptiveness, he found she was one of the few people he actually enjoyed talking with.

They hung up with Noah promising to call her in the morning.

Turns out his father wanted him up for breakfast. Whereas most of his friend's fathers took them out duck or deer hunting or even fishing before daylight, Noah's father took him to the country club for breakfast.

Noah had an ominous feeling that day.

"Son," his father said, with next to no preamble after they ordered. "I want you to marry Claire."

Noah felt the bottom fell out from under him.

The problem with his father was that Martin Worthington got what he wanted. And Noah knew that when his father wanted something, no matter how much he protested, it still happened.

"I don't want to marry Claire. I'm going to marry Savannah."

His father waved him off. "You can use the company plane to go see Savannah whenever you want, but I need you to marry Claire."

"I don't understand," Noah protested. "Why would I possibly want to marry… her?"

"You don't have to want to marry her," his father insisted. "Do you think I married your mother for love?"

"I kind of thought so,"

"Of course not. Men in our position make the most of every opportunity."

Noah shook his head. "Not marriage."

His father sighed. "Let me lay it out for you. With you marrying Claire, her father and I will merge our companies."

"Just merge them without me."

"It doesn't work like that, son. You're the incentive. Our family name is what he's after."

Noah gaped at his father. This was a new level.

"There's plenty in it for you," his father continued, digging into his omelet. "You'll have your own company plane and be over the other pilots. You'll be able to choose which trips you take."

"I have other job offers," Noah insisted. "that don't require me to marry someone I don't love."

"You can take the plane to see Savannah whenever you want. Until you get tired of her."

Noah glared at his father. "No," he said.

"The alternative," his father continued, "is that your mother and I disinherit you. You get nothing from this day forward."

Noah dismissed it. "Mother wouldn't do that."

His father put down his fork, reached into his coat pocket and pulled out a folded, notarized document. Taking his time, keeping his eyes on his son's, he unfolded the papers and laid them on the table in front of Noah.

Noah broke his father's gaze and looked down at the signed document. His mother's signature – disinheriting her only child. The money going to charity upon his father's death with a small stipend going to take care of his mother unless she remarried.

Noah glared at his father in disbelief. His father merely smirked.

Noah pushed back his chair and stood up. His fists clenched reflexively. He would never hit his father. But this was one time in his life when he was tempted.

Grabbing the document, he turned and stalked away. He couldn't look at his father. The man disgusted him.

Going outside, he started walking. He just needed to get away.

Ridiculous. His father's demand was insane. Why would he possibly agree to do it?

He didn't need his father's money. He could get his own job. He didn't have to be rich. He just wanted to be happy. And he was happy. He loved Savannah. There would never be anyone else for him.

His flash of anger settling, he stopped and sat on a park bench. Stared at the golfers hitting their little balls. Plotting their businesses. Ruining people's lives.

No. He did not want to be – would not be – part of this world.

Able to focus a little better now, he began reading the four-page document.

When he was finished reading, he knew he didn't have a choice.

He had to marry Claire Beauchamp.

4

Savannah excused herself from the dinner table and went to the ladies' room. She paced a bit in the parlor area, then perched on one of the oversized chairs. Got up and paced some more.

What she took from Noah's story was that he had fought for her. But his father had been too much. Too powerful.

The bottom line was that Noah had been forced to choose between her and his inheritance.

He had chosen his inheritance.

She had to respect him for that.

Didn't she?

He could have talked to her about it. Explained that he needed to marry someone else or his father would disinherit him.

Savannah scoffed and put her head in her hands.

A woman, old enough to be her mother, placed a hand lightly on Savannah's shoulder. "Are you alright, Dear?"

Savannah looked at the older woman. Forced herself to smile. "Yes. Thank you. I'm just trying to sort something out."

The woman apologized for bothering her and left.

Savannah knew that Noah knew that she never would have understood. The result had been the same. Perhaps it was best that he never contacted her again.

She had looked for him.

Watched for him even. Stayed home on the weekends, studying. Secretly waiting for the phone to ring.

He should have at least told me.

But he hadn't.

And life had gone on.

She wanted to hear the rest of how he got to where he was now.

Checking her appearance in the mirror, deeming herself presentable, she went back out to the table where Noah waited for her. His expression anxious.

"Are you alright?" he asked.

"I'm good. I just needed to take a moment." She gulped the rest of her wine. "So, did you do it? Did you marry Claire?"

"I did. It was fast. Two weeks after I got back, I was married," he lowered his gaze. "I couldn't tell you. As long as I didn't tell you, it wasn't real. Any day, I thought, I would wake up and it would have all been a nightmare. And I was so ashamed. Ashamed that I had let my father decide who I was to marry."

"I can see where you would be."

"Yeah," he ran a hand through his hair. Savannah could see the pain his eyes. After all this time it was still there. "I married her, but it was in name only."

She watched him carefully.

"Anyway, we had separate bedrooms. The day we got back from the honeymoon I told her I was going to work for the airline. She got mad and it made avoiding her easier from there on out."

"But you stayed married."

"We did. We'll be divorced soon though."

"Why now?"

"My father died eighteen months ago. My mother and I own everything now."

"Rather ironic, isn't it?"

"Hmm. I refused to spend any of his money while he lived."

"You were really angry."

"I never forgave him. He destroyed my relationship with you."

"I am so sorry."

"Don't be sorry. I made my choice."

"You didn't really have a choice."

"Looking back, I think he was bluffing. I don't think he would have done that. But, I was young and couldn't imagine living without the money I'd grown up with."

"You made what seemed to be the best decision at the time."

"You always were understanding. I knew that. But I didn't think even you could handle what I was doing."

"I don't think I could have. The end result would have been the same. Except that I would have known what happened. I actually thought I did something wrong – something to make you stop loving me."

"You were perfect. I would never do that to you now. I hope you can find your way around to forgiving me."

She nodded. Did she forgive him? Even if she did, she couldn't bring herself to say the words right now.

The server brought their meals which lightened the mood somewhat. Savannah had liked it better before they'd dug into their pasts. Noah had been right to avoid the topic.

"You were right," she told him.

"That's always good to hear. What was I right about?"

"It was too soon to talk about all that."

"It's out there now," he said. "Can I change the subject?"

"Please."

"How do you like your tour of New York so far?"

That brought a smile to her face. "I like it very much."

"Good. Does that mean you're available for tomorrow?"

She nodded, taking a bite of fish.

"There is one requirement. You have to wear jeans and flat shoes that you can walk in."

"I can do that," she said.

They finished eating in silence. Now that Savannah had a little information regarding his past, her brain began to focus on the future. Was he going to just show her around New York, then disappear again? Was this his way of atoning for his past?

She still felt that pull toward him. That dangerous pull. Dangerous because the pull was at her heart.

It had always been there.

She allowed her mind to wander. He had filled out in the last twenty years. She'd always felt safe around him. That hadn't changed. Last night when he'd held her against him, it had felt right.

He was keeping her at arm's length, nonetheless. It would be so easy to slip back into that close physical relationship. What was holding him back? Was he no longer interested in her that way?

She watched him under her lashes. Longed to feel his lips against hers again.

In the year they had been together, they'd spent countless hours with their lips locked together. They had never gone all the way though. They had agreed that they should wait. She had only been a college freshman. If they had, would it have changed anything?

They hadn't talked about marriage. They had just… been in the relationship. Savannah hadn't questioned the future.

But now…

Now she wanted to know. She wanted to know how much to invest in him. It had been two days now and he hadn't even tried to kiss her.

"Do you still like mint chocolate chip ice cream?"

Her jaw dropped. "You remember that?"

"I remember a lot of things," he said, placing a hand over hers, his eyes twinkling with mischief.

"I haven't had it in so long, I really don't know," she said, her thoughts scattered with the feel of his hand over hers.

"There's an ice-cream parlor around the corner if you'd like to find out."

"Ok," she said simply.

He paid the check and they got on the elevator to go downstairs."

Since it wasn't far to the ice cream shop, they walked along the sidewalk. Steam from the subways drifted up creating a unique urban fog.

It reminded Savannah of their long walks along Lake Martin after the rains.

"Do you remember," she asked, "when you had me out on the lake hunting for frogs?"

He stopped. Looked at her and broke out into a deep male laugh. "What on earth made you remember that? While walking downtown New York?"

"The fog," she said, and he laughed harder. "What?"

"Fog," he said, bent over now.

"Steam. Whatever," she said, biting her lip to try to keep from laughing with him. It wasn't long before they were both walking hand in hand down the sidewalk laughing at a joke only the two of them could fathom.

"It wasn't my idea," he said. "Johnny Ray told me that girls were impressed by guys who could catch frogs."

"What? Please tell me you're kidding."

"Scout's honor," he held up his hand.

"I'm not concerned about what he told you. I'm concerned about the fact that you believed him."

"I didn't know. He said it was an Alabama thing. I was from Ft. Worth. It seemed possible at the time."

"Do I look like the kind of girl who would be impressed by her boyfriend catching frogs?"

"Well, no, not now."

"I think you should have just said no and let it go at that."

"I didn't know you all that well at the time."

"Oh, my. I can't believe you were trying to impress me. I thought you were just some country guy dragging me out to look for frogs."

"I guess it's a good thing we didn't find one."

"Probably. Especially if you thought I'd know what to do with it."

"He said you'd know."

"Johnny Ray was an idiot."

"He's an attorney now."

"No way! You stayed in touch with him?"

"Sort of. He calls about once a year."

"Well, you can tell him, attorney or no, he's an idiot."

"Turns out he's not a bad attorney."

"I never would have guessed that."

They arrived at the ice cream parlor and stood in line. They were the oldest ones there. The clientele consisted mostly of young couples.

"We used to be like that," she said, without thinking.

He put his arm around her, pulled her close. "We still are. Actually, we're better. We can take any one of these couples."

"Take them how?"

He squeezed her close. "I don't know. It just sounds good."

"One scoop or two?" he asked when they got to the counter.

"One," she said.

He ordered her a scoop of mint chocolate chip and he ordered a two scoops of fudge swirl vanilla.

They found a bench and sat side by side.

"Is it as good as you remember?" he asked.

"It's even better," she said, licking her spoon.

"Mine too," he said, "Here, try a bite."

Without even thinking, she allowed him to feed her a bite of his ice cream. "That's good, too," she said, holding her spoon out to him to try hers.

"Not bad."

She was reminded that they had shared pretty much everything. She couldn't imagine that there were two other people more attached at the hip than they had been back in college.

She gazed at him. He smiled.

It was though a piece of her had been missing all those twenty years.

And here was the missing piece.

She'd been hurt. There was no denying that. But in that moment, sitting outside a New York ice cream parlor surrounded by young people, many of whom were the same age they had been, she realized that she forgave him.

They were different people now. Yet they were the same. It was odd how after twenty years, they still fit together so well. Despite the changes each had undergone.

She smiled back at him. "Thank you," she said. "Thank you for showing me the fun side of New York."

"It is my honor," he said.

His lips cold from the ice cream, he bent over and kissed her cheek, only a fraction from the corner of her mouth.

Her nerve endings went on edge. And craved more. She wanted more. She wanted to feel his lips against hers. Instead, she settled for another bite of ice cream.

And wondered.

After all this time, when would the time be right to begin again?

. . .

SUNDAY IN THE PARK.

Although Savannah knew the lyrics to the Chicago song were actually Saturday in the park, she changed the words around to fit Sunday in her head as she sang silently to herself.

They'd started off with a hot dog from the hot dog stand. Then boarded the Staten Island ferry.

The sky was clear. The breeze was perfect.

The day was perfect.

They had to wait in line after a long walk to the Statue. Thank goodness for flat ballerina shoes.

"She's so… big," she said, looking up at Lady Liberty.

"The tall buildings of New York make her look small, but in her day, she was huge."

"From where I'm standing, she still is."

There was a middle-aged couple in line in front of them. The woman turned around, smiled at them. "Make sure you go up to the crown," the woman said. "We come here every year and until last year, we never remembered to get advance tickets. You can't go without advance tickets. And there's always a long line. But last year, we remembered and decided to wait it out. It was so worth it."

"How long is the wait?"

"It was what, honey, about two hours?"

"I don't know," the man said. "I just remember we missed lunch. So we made sure we ate before we came out today. And it's really strenuous."

"Oh, yes, "Sue added. "You only want to wear comfortable shoes."

"You come every year?" Savannah asked. "Where are you from?"

"We live in Pittsburgh."

"I've been there. It's a really pretty city."

The woman nodded. "You know, Honey," she said to her

husband. "Would you go get me bottle of water?" She turned to Savannah. "I'm diabetic, so I have to keep hydrated."

The man looked at Noah. "Want to come with me to get water?"

Noah looked questioningly at Savannah. "Do you want some water?"

"Actually, yes, I really do."

"You'll be ok here?"

"Sure," she said, waving her hand.

While Noah was gone to get water, Savannah learned that Sue and Mike were not originally from Pittsburgh. Sue was from Iowa and Mike was from Arizona. They'd met while in school at the University of Pittsburgh. Then had decided to stay.

"But enough about us," Sue said as the line inched painfully forward. Savannah could see Noah in line at the concession stand.

"Where are you two from?"

"Birmingham," Savannah said, keeping things simple.

"You're such a cute couple. How long have you been married?"

"Oh, we're not," Savannah said, relieved to see that Noah and Mike were on their way back

"Really?"

"No. But we've known each other forever, Since college actually."

"That's the best way to start a relationship – as friends."

Savannah wanted to say that she and Noah had never been friends. Instead, she smiled and nodded.

But the thought startled her a little.

Noah had been it for her since the day they met.

Being with him like this, now.

This uncertainty.

Was dangerous territory for her.

A few minutes later, when she and Noah had a moment of privacy, Noah took the tickets out of his pocket and handed them to her.

They had advance tickets to go up the Statue of Liberty's crown.

Dangerous territory indeed.

5

SAVANNAH – BEFORE

She was here.

She was actually doing this.

She was a freshman at college.

She waited in the registration line with Betty, her friend from high school.

Betty was what Savannah's mom called boy crazy. Even now, Betty had already pointed out three different guys that she'd like to go out with. And they'd only been here for thirty minutes.

Savannah wasn't looking at boys. Savannah was worried about whether her classes would be filled by the time they finally got up to the registration desk. Being first-time freshmen, they didn't exactly get first pick of class times.

By the time they got to the front of the line, Betty had struck up a conversation with a guy standing next to her.

"Next."

Betty waved Savannah off. "You go ahead," she said. "I'll take the next one."

Eager to get enrolled, so they could hit the bookstore, Savannah didn't hesitate to go ahead.

Registration was completed in booths manned by older students. She went up to the upperclassman and, her hands shaking, handed him the form that had been signed by her advisor.

"You can sit down," the student worker told her.

She sat on the edge of the seat and watched as he typed in her information.

"Savannah Skye Richards," he said.

She nodded, glanced at him and returned her eyes to the screen.

"From Birmingham."

"Yes."

"That's only, what, a couple hours away? So you'll be commuting?"

"No," she said, "I'll be living on campus."

"That's good." He clicked the keys. "Your English is closed."

"Oh no," she groaned.

"And your math."

She felt the tears welling in her eyes. Here she was, ready to start classes and couldn't even get in.

"Hey," he said, "your biology is good. And I got you in the psychology class. Let me check the history."

She held her breath.

"Closed."

"What do I do?" she asked. "I only have two classes?"

"Oh no. We're not finished," he said, watching her carefully.

I won't cry, she repeated over and over to herself.

"I can move your history to 9:00, so that's done." He clicked deftly on the computer keyboard. "Then I can put you in the 2:00 English. So I just switched those two out. You'll like this English professor better. Trust me."

She turned her eyes to his. And was mesmerized by the deep blue. His smile was kind.

"What about my math?" she asked, a glimmer of hope shooting through her.

"Math always fills up quick," he said, "Even though no one wants to take it. I've yet to meet anyone who actually likes math."

"I like math," she said, her voice no more than a whisper.

"No kidding?"

"Yeah. I went to state."

"No way," he said. "How did you do?"

"First place," She began to relax a bit.

He looked back at the computer. "There is seriously nothing open."

She really needed the math. She had her whole schedule worked out and math was a prerequisite that would put her whole schedule behind.

"Hold on a minute." He picked up the phone. Spoke briefly to someone on the other end. More tapping on the keyboard. "Alright," he said. "You are in."

"But how?"

"I got you an override."

"You can do that?"

"I've found that if I ask only about once every now and then, they realize how important it must be and give it to me."

He gestured over to the booth next to him where Betty now sat. "She calls ALL the time and only rarely gets an override."

Poor Betty.

He hit print and said, "I'll be right back,"

Savannah waited, much calmer now. She was ready to hit the bookstore.

He came back, handed her a printout of her schedule. "Just what you wanted. I only had to switch out two classes, but your times are the same."

Savannah studied her schedule. Looked up and smiled. "Thank you so much."

"I'm happy I could help." He seemed to consider.

"Is this it? What do I do now?"

"The next stop is fee payment." He leaned back, his expression quizzical. "There is one other thing."

She looked at him questioningly.

"I'm supposed to go to the orientation dance on Friday."

She knew there were lots of activities this week, but hadn't paid much attention. "Ok."

He laughed. "Will you go with me?"

"I don't usually go to dances."

"I don't either," he said. "But I kind of have to go to this one. And it's a good excuse to get to know you better."

"I'm just a regular freshman."

"I have a feeling you're anything but regular. So what do you say? Can I be your escort to the dance?"

"I don't know," she said. "Maybe I'll meet you there if I go."

He swirled around, picked up a flyer from his desk. Handed it to her. "If you change your mind, this is where I'll be."

She took the flyer. Glanced at it. "I don't even know your name," she said.

He pointed to his Auburn University name tag. "Noah," he said. "I'm fully vetted." Then, as though on impulse, he took the flyer back from her, scribbled his name and a phone number. Handed it back to her. "I'll walk you to your next station," he said, standing up.

She stood up. "I have to wait for Betty," she said, glancing at the line of students waiting for their turn at registration. "Besides," she said. "I think you have a line."

"All right," he said, "you win. See you Friday Savannah Skye."

Betty walked up at that moment. "What happens Friday?" she asked.

"Nothing," Savannah said, turning and steering her friend away.

"What? Do you have a date with Mr. Hunk?"

"Mr. who? No. I don't date."

"Then what?" Betty saw the flyer clutched in her friend's hand, lifted it enough to see the header. "He invited you to the dance?"

"Yeah," she said. "I can't go."

Betty grinned from ear to ear. "What do you mean you can't go? We're freshmen. We have to go."

"We don't have to go anywhere but class."

Betty glued her feet to the ground. "Savannah, president of the high school student class, is not going to go to college and be a hermit."

"I'm not a hermit."

"Sounds like it. If Mr. Hunky guy asked me to go to my own dance with him, I would most certainly go."

"You would go if anyone asked."

Betty's eyes widened.

"I'll think about it," Savannah acquiesced.

Betty frowned, but started walking again. "I guess that's something at least."

Later that evening, Savannah sat in her new dorm room and arranged her desk. Betty, also her roommate, was out, somewhere, with a group of girls who had come by recruiting freshmen. Savannah had waved them off, not paying much attention to where they were going.

She turned on her little lamp and opened each one of her textbooks, thumbing through them in anticipation of the worlds of knowledge they held.

She settled on her biology text and started reading.

After a few minutes, she laughed at herself. Studying the week before classes even began. She got up, stretched, and went to the refrigerator for a soda.

Betty had tacked the dance flyer to the front of the fridge. Savannah took it down, read it for at least the tenth time, and stared at Noah's name and phone number. A number she had memorized.

She hadn't gone on a date since her high school prom. Her date, Timothy had gotten drunk, and decided he really wanted to be dancing with Mark. Granted, Mark was a good-looking guy.

But something about having one's high school prom date coming out on the night of the prom had left her with a slight aversion to dating.

Savannah had never been "boy crazy" anyway. Not that she didn't like boys. She just preferred to be a little more selective. In fact, she never would have gone to the prom with Timothy if Betty hadn't insisted that they should double date.

Noah had seemed nice, but she really didn't have the time to even be thinking about a boy, much less spending time with one.

No, she decided, putting the flyer back on the refrigerator, she definitely would not be going to the orientation dance.

TWO NIGHTS LATER, Savannah followed Betty into the student union.

Against her better judgment.

"I really don't do dances," she said to Betty for what must have been the fifteenth time, that night alone.

"I know. I was there when the whole senior prom thing fell apart. If anyone is qualified to keep you away from dances, it's me. But this is college," Betty insisted. "You have to move on. Get back on the horse."

Savannah kept her comments to herself. Betty had been dogging her for two days now. She ran her hands along her jeans. Straightened the sleeves of her pink polo. She was actually a little nervous.

She'd agreed to come along to keep Betty company. She

didn't like the idea of her friend walking around campus at night by herself. *I've really got to get past this. I can't follow Betty around for four years.*

She justified her decision to come along with the newness of college for both of them. As they entered the room, she found herself searching for a glimpse of Noah. Would he really be there? He was an upperclassman. Why would he be at a freshman dance?

Betty went to the check-in desk and presented her ID.

"Savannah," Betty said, tugging at Savannah's sleeve. "Show the guy your ID."

Savannah pulled her ID out of her back pocket and, after glancing at her friend who was grinning like a Cheshire cat, presented her ID.

To Noah.

"Hello Savannah Skye Richards," he said, without looking at her ID card.

She felt the flush in her cheeks. The very person she'd been searching for was sitting right in front of her.

He leaned over, whispered something to the girl sitting to him, and pushed back his chair. He was tall – at least six feet. He came around the table, nodded to Betty. "I'll show you around," he said, turning his attention back to Savannah.

"I'll get something to drink," Betty said, bouncing off toward the concession area.

Frowning, Savannah watched her friend desert her.

"I wasn't sure I'd ever see you again," he said.

She met his gaze. "You had my address, not to mention my class schedule."

"True," he said, "But that would be stalking. I'm not saying I never would have used it, but I was hoping not to have to."

"Why?" she asked simply.

"You're the only girl I ever met who likes math."

She scoffed, turned away. "That's not a good reason."

"Ok," he said, putting his hands up. "You got me. I don't have a reason."

She turned back to him. "You're a strange man, Noah Worthington."

He broke into a wide smile.

She couldn't help it. She smiled back.

"Savannah," he said, taking her hand. "Just give me a chance."

With Chicago blasting in the background, they made their way around the crowded floor to an empty table.

"Aren't you supposed to be working?" she asked, leaning close so he could hear.

"I was just here to help out if they need anything. It was just an excuse so I wouldn't look like a weirdo stalking freshman girls. So I was hanging out. Waiting for someone to show up."

"Just anyone."

"No, I had the possibility of a date."

"What were you going to do if I didn't show up?"

"I was planning to stay about thirty more minutes, then head home. I didn't think you were coming."

"I wasn't."

"But you're here."

"I just came to keep Betty from being out after dark by herself."

"You really know how to boost a guy's ego."

She laughed. "Sorry."

"It's ok."

"You don't have a girlfriend?"

"No."

"Are you a senior?"

He nodded "It's my last year."

"In..."

"Aviation."

Noah had been cool before, but now he was… out of her league.

"You should definitely have a girlfriend."

"I agree."

"But not a freshman just out of high school."

"I don't see anything but college girls here."

Her lips curved into a smile. "I suppose you're right," she said. "However, I maintain my stance."

"Tell me your major again."

"I'm undeclared."

"That's what I thought," he said. "And as a very wise senior, I think you should declare a very lofty major."

"Something akin to aviation?"

"Nah. You're not the mechanic type. You need something more abstract. Like law."

"My uncle's a lawyer. It's overrated."

"How about psychology?"

"Maybe," she said. "I looked at it. But there's only one math."

"Yeah, the math thing. They have statistics."

"I'll keep it in mind."

"You'll figure it out."

"Yes, I will."

"I don't want to spend our whole first date talking shop."

"When did this become a date?" She looked around at the awkward freshmen, just getting their footing in the college world.

When he didn't answer, she turned back. His face was ever so close. He placed his fingers on her cheek and his thumb next to her mouth. Then his lips were pressed softly against hers.

Time froze as she absorbed the sensation of having his lips against hers and his fingertips on her skin.

As the Chicago song ended and faded into the next, he pulled back. "Now," he said. "Now it's a date."

6

Savannah's phone vibrated. She glanced at it. Groaned. "It's my mom," she said.

"Answer it," Noah said, slathering marmalade on a slice of toast.

"I'll call her back," Savannah said. "How can you eat all that sugar?" she asked, picking up a cluster of grapes, pulling one off and popping it into her mouth.

"You should really try it," he said, breaking off a piece of toast and handing it to her.

She took and tasted. "Too sweet," she said.

"I don't see how you do it. I could never live without sugar."

"If," she began, but picked up her phone. It was her mother again. Twice in a row. "Hello."

"Savannah," her mother said, her voice shaky.

"What is it?" Savannah said, turning, walking toward the balcony, her heart racing.

"The house was robbed."

"What? What do you mean? Are you hurt?"

"No, I wasn't home. I came home and the front door was open."

"Thank God you weren't hurt."

"Savannah," her mother sniffed. "Whiskers is gone."

Savannah had watched her mother bury her father. Her eyes red from crying. Other than that one time, never, not once had she heard her mother upset like this.

"What do you mean he's gone?"

"The front door was open and I can't find him anywhere."

Whiskers was her mother's fifteen-year-old cat. Whiskers had never put his feet on the ground outside.

"Did you look everywhere? Maybe he's hiding."

"He's not here. I looked everywhere."

"You'll find him, Mom."

"I called and called. The police looked for him, too. When are you coming home?"

"My flight doesn't leave until 9:00 in the morning. Where's Charlotte?"

"Your sister went somewhere with the school on a bus. She can't come."

"Mom, I'm in New York."

"I know. I just don't know what else to do."

Savannah had to do something. She couldn't bear to see her mother like this. "Did you check with the neighbors?"

"I checked with everyone. I'm only calling you because I don't know what else to do."

Savannah put the phone away from her ear, looked back at Noah. He'd stood up and was watching her.

"Can I help?" he asked.

"My mom's house was robbed and the cat got out. She can't find him."

She put the phone back to her ear. Her mother was sobbing. "I can't lose Whiskers. Your father and I raised him from a little kitten."

"I know, Mom. Let me call the airline. I'll see if I can get back sooner. I'll call you back. Just hold on ok. We'll find him."

She hung up and paced for a moment before turning around. "It's funny, huh? I can handle almost any crisis except when it comes to my family."

"Seems normal to me," he said, going to her. He pulled her against him, hugged her, and released her.

"You need to get home," he said.

She nodded. "I have to call the airline."

"Wait," he said. "I can… um. I have some pull. I can get you home."

"Alright."

"How soon can you be packed and ready?"

She had showered and dressed before he came to her room for breakfast. She was used to packing, so it never took her long to get out of a hotel. "I need thirty minutes," she said.

"Good," he said. "I'll make a call, grab my things, and be back here in thirty."

As he headed out the door, Savannah called her mother back. Assured her that she was on her way. Her mother sounded a little calmer now. Having heard her mother in a hysterical state only one other time, it was almost Savannah's undoing. "I don't know how I can help," she said, putting her mother on speaker while she tossed her clothes into her suitcase and gathered her things from the bathroom.

"Just get here and help me look for him."

"I'll call you when I know my ETA."

After hanging up, she scanned the room, stood her luggage next to the door, and went to stand in front of the dresser where the roses sat. She pulled out the single rose with the white ribbon tied around it. Dried it with a towel, and took it with her.

They hadn't time to wait for a bellhop, so when Noah returned, he had a luggage cart with him. She had no idea how he had gotten to his room and back, packed, arranged a flight, and located a cart, all in thirty minutes. It didn't matter. He was here and she was grateful.

He stacked their luggage on the cart and they made their way out to a taxi.

"How is she?" he asked once they were loaded into the vehicle and on their way to the airport.

"Hysterical."

"I don't remember your mother being the hysterical type."

"Exactly. That's what's so disconcerting about the whole thing."

"What did they take?"

"The robbers? She didn't even say. I don't think she cares. All they had to do was close the door behind them. And not let the cat out."

"She's had this cat a long time."

"Fifteen years. He's part of the family. He's a cool cat though. He talks."

"Is that so? That is special."

She laughed. Felt her eyes tearing up. "Poor little guy."

Noah took her hand. She held it a moment, but had too much nervous energy. "When does my flight leave?"

"Our flight leaves when we get to the airport."

"Our?"

"I'm going with you."

"No," she said, but felt her phone vibrating. "I'm on my way to the airport, Mom."

"Thank God. I'm going to go sit out back and wait. In case he comes home."

"What did they take?"

"I don't know. Nothing important."

"I'm glad you weren't home."

"If I'd been home, Whiskers wouldn't be out there."

"Mom?"

"What?"

"Never mind. I have to hang up now, but I'll call you when I land." She hung up the phone. "I hope they didn't take Whiskers."

"I take it your mom hasn't thought of that."

"Apparently not. God help them if she finds out who did this. Especially if they hurt her cat."

"No kidding."

"You don't have to go with me," she said.

His lips curved into an odd smile. "I kind of do have to."

She kind of didn't understand why he thought so, but her mind was preoccupied, so she let it go.

The taxi driver didn't stop at any of the gates. "Which airline are we flying?" she asked.

He shook his head.

Savannah began ticking off in her head what she could do when she got to her mother's house. They could make signs with Whisker's picture on them and plaster them around the neighborhood. She scrolled through her photos looking for a picture of Whiskers. They needed to call the local vets. Alert them. She was fairly certain Whiskers had a locater chip. Especially if he was stolen, they needed to be on the lookout.

Noah spoke briefly on the phone, but she tuned him out as he spoke flight jargon.

Her mind preoccupied, focused on her phone, she followed him out of the taxi, waited while their luggage was unloaded. Her suitcase rolling alongside her, she finally looked up. Squinted in the sunlight.

"We have to walk a little," Noah said.

Savannah looked around. And followed him toward a small jet sitting alone on the runway.

"You hired a private jet?" she asked, stopping to stare at him.

"No," he said. "I'm a pilot, remember?"

"They let you use planes whenever you want?" Truly, there was so much about the aviation industry that she was clueless about.

"Something like that," he said. "Come on, we're cleared to get on the runway."

The flight assistant took their luggage, tucked it away. Noah helped her up the stairs into the plane.

The plane smelled new. Like a new car.

She turned right to go into the cabin. There was no else on board.

"You can sit back there," he said. She stopped and looked at him. He nodded toward the back of the plane. "Or you can sit up here," he said, turning his head toward the cockpit.

She frowned. Why would she want to do that?

"With me," he said.

Her feet were glued to the floor. She wasn't sure which way to go.

Her gaze locked onto his. On the pleased smile on his face.

And everything she knew about Noah clicked into place.

His passion for flying.

The story he'd told her about his father.

Her face broke into a wide smile. "This is your plane."

His expression was not what she expected. It was more like a deer in headlights. "But you didn't want me to know that."

He squared his shoulders, shook his head, and returned her smile. "Nothing gets past you, Savannah Richards. Come on," he held out his hand.

If not for her mother's plight, Savannah's excitement would have been uncontrollable. She sat down in the co-pilot's seat, took the headset from him, and nearly bounced in her seat. "It looks a lot different than it used to look," she said. The cockpit was all glass, providing a clean view of everything. Gone were the old round dials and gauges. Everything was displayed on what looked like three large computer screens.

"That was a long time ago," he said after she pointed that out to him, "and this is a much better plane." The pride in his voice was evident.

"It is yours then?"

He winked at her as he put his own headset on. "All mine."

7

Savannah had flown with Noah before, but always in little prop planes. This was different. Faster. Higher. Not so loud.

They could actually talk without wearing headsets.

He put the plane on autopilot and leaned back to get them bottles of water. Savannah stared nervously out the window.

His attention was only off a few seconds, but her imagination was nearly her undoing.

One look at her face as he turned back, handing her the bottle of water, was all it took. "I can see that I'm going to have to teach you to fly so you won't panic."

"I think it's best if you just keep our hands on the wheel."

He laughed. "All right, but…" he gestured toward the empty sky. "There's not exactly a lot to run into up here."

"Easy for you to say," she said. "You never know when some crazy driver will come out of nowhere."

"If another plane comes within a hundred miles, all sorts of alarms start to go off."

"Really?"

"Well, no, but it sounds good. We have our own flight path and no one else should be near us."

"What if someone deviates?"

He shook his head. "It rarely happens."

"Rarely."

"When did you become such a nervous flyer?"

"I watch too much TV."

He looked at her, disbelief evident.

"I do fly a lot, but it's different up here. Up front."

"You get used to it."

"I don't think that's a good idea. I could never afford private charter fees."

"You'll never pay a fee with me," he said matter-of-factly, his attention focused on the computers.

His words brought a little flush to her cheeks, and some unexpected emotion. Fortunately, he was busy checking the displays and didn't notice.

Despite her occasional anxieties, the flight was uneventful. Noah assured her that an uneventful flight was the ultimate goal.

After they landed at the Birmingham airport, Noah secured a car. "They keep cars on hand for us to use while we're here," he explained.

"Yeah, that part I remembered," she said, but he was busy signing some paperwork and didn't seem to hear. How many times had they dashed to a town, took a car to get a burger and dashed back to the plane to fly home? That wasn't exactly something a girl could easily forget.

He retrieved their luggage and together they rolled their bags to the borrowed car.

Savannah checked her phone. No calls from her mother. No calls from anyone.

"No news is good news," he said. "right?"

"Not with my mother. She may be in full blown crisis mode by now."

"That thought terrifies me."

"Ha. You and me both."

When they pulled up to her mother's house, there was still a cop car in the driveway. Her mother lived a suburban cul-de-sac in a white Victorian style home with four dormer windows across the third story. The house had been built when Savannah was an infant. She'd lived there until she went away for college at eighteen.

A little sliver of panic shot through her as the memory of driving up to her parents' house two years after Noah left came back in a flash. There had been an ambulance and three cop cars in the drive way, their lights shattering the peaceful night air.

Her mother had called her cell phone, while she sat in a night class, focused on neurotransmitters and the myelin sheath – something she had never forgotten. She'd been hysterical – waiting on the ambulance to come and save her father from a heart attack. Unfortunately, they had gotten there too late and by the time Savannah pulled up to the house, they had her father in the ambulance. They had not been able to save him. Her mother sat on the front steps, her head in her hands.

"Savannah?" Noah asked.

"I'm sorry," she said, trying to smile. Pulling herself back to the present. Her mother's house had been broken into and Whiskers was missing. No one was dying.

"Tell me," he said.

"My father died two years after you left from a heart attack. I was just… I was just…"

"I didn't know. I'm so sorry."

"It was a long time ago."

"It may have been, but you don't just get over something like that."

"Let's check on Mom and see if we can find Whiskers." She jumped out of the car and rushed inside, her heart racing in spite of telling herself she was overreacting.

Normally, she would have knocked, but the door was unlocked. Her mother was sitting on the sofa talking to the policeman when Savannah walked in. As usual, her mother, who did cardio daily, and could easily wear Savannah's clothes, was impeccably dressed in black slacks with low pumps and a deep emerald tunic. She had recently cut her hair to her chin, and it bounced healthily against her cheek as she shook her head.

She got up when she saw Savannah and drew her into a hug, holding her as though she wouldn't let her go. "I'm so glad you're here," she said.

"Whiskers?" Savannah asked, pulling back to meet her mother's gaze.

Her mother's eyes glistened with unshed tears. "I've looked everywhere."

"I'll look for him," Savannah said, desperate to remove the agony from her mother's face. "Mom," she turned to Noah. "this is…"

"Hello Noah," her mother said. "Please sit wherever you like. The officer is just leaving."

Noah obediently sat on the edge of the loveseat and waited.

Savannah began looking for the cat, first checking under the sofa. It was as though her mother just saw Noah last week, not twenty years ago. How could she not show at least a little surprise? Savannah would have to think about that later. It was too overwhelming to think about at the moment.

After her mother saw the officer out and returned to the living room, she went up to Noah and hugged him, too.

"You don't seem surprised to see me, Mrs. Richards," he said.

She shrugged. "I knew you'd be back. It was just a matter of time. Please, call me Emily."

Savannah moved her search upstairs and Emily followed behind her. After Savannah had searched every inch of the house for a place a cat could hide, they went back to the living room where Noah waited.

"Which door was left open?" she asked.

"The back door. Did they take anything?" *Other than Whiskers.*

"I don't think so. I don't have any valuables just lying around. Anything valuable is in your father's gun safe."

"Did they take his guns?"

"No, it looks like they tried to pry it open though."

Savannah held out her hand to Noah. "We're gonna go out back and look around for few minutes."

"Go ahead. I've looked everywhere. I'm gonna call your sister again."

Savannah led Noah out the back door. And they sat on the big porch swing, not touching, but only inches apart. Savannah was flooded with memories of them doing more than sitting out here.

"Whiskers must be pretty scared," Noah commented, seemingly unaffected by such memories.

"I'm sure." She scanned the yard, looking for any sign whatsoever of the white Persian cat.

"Has he ever been outside before?"

"I don't think his feet have ever touched the ground."

"Did you tell her I was coming?"

Savannah turned and focused her attention on Noah. "I hadn't even told her that we ran into each other, much less that you were coming with me."

"That's odd."

"It's very odd."

"Did you ever talk about me?"

Savannah frowned.

"I mean, it's just weird that she reacted like that."

"She's stressed out. Anyway, you never know what she's going to say. I wouldn't worry too much about it."

"It's almost like it was yesterday and not twenty years ago."

She laughed. "I'm telling you, you'll drive yourself in circles if you keep trying to figure it out."

"I'll ask her about it."

"She always liked you."

"Really?" His face lit up.

"Of course. My dad liked you too."

"That's good to know. You two were close."

"Our family was close-knit. My sister, though, is more like my mom. A little 'odd' as you would say. I'm more like my dad. More scientific."

"Wasn't he a professor?"

"Good memory."

"I remember him being kind of quiet, but always very polite"

"That's my dad. Quiet and polite."

"You're kind of a cross between your two parents."

"Thank you," wondering if that had been a compliment. Her mother could be a little difficult at times.

She got up, went to stand at the edge of the porch and looked toward what had been her father's tool shed.

She squinted. Something moved.

Could it be?

She dashed down the stairs, across the lawn, toward the tool shed. Huddled there, next to the edge of the tool shed, was a bright-eyed white cat. "Whiskers!" she said, walking slowly, so as not to spook him.

He stood up, swished his tail in the air, and walked toward

her. Reaching down, she picked him up and held him close as he clung to her shoulder. Noah watched her from the top step.

"Where have you been, little guy?" she asked. "Your mommy is going to be so happy."

"I take it this is Whiskers," Noah said, opening the back door for them.

"This is Whiskers. The one we flew all the way from New York to find."

Once Emily and Whiskers were reunited, Savannah and Noah sat side by side, again, not touching, but only inches apart, on the sofa.

"What do we do now?" he asked.

She shrugged. Hugged a blue throw pillow to her.

"Do you want to go back to New York?"

"Not right now. I'm a little tired."

"Come here," he said, shifting to rub her shoulders. As he massaged the tension from her neck, she moaned softly.

"Good?"

"You have no idea."

"Ok," Emily said, coming into the room. "I have the guest room ready. You two can sleep there tonight."

"Oh, um." Savannah was torn between coherent thought and the feel of Noah's hands on her neck and shoulders. "We don't sleep in the same room."

Her mother narrowed her eyes in that way only mothers could do. "Well, I suppose you'll work it out."

Noah stopped and sat back. Savannah's head began to clear. "What about one of the other rooms?"

"Your sister's room is the process of being painted and there's no bed in there anyway. I made the other guest room into my hobby room."

"Maybe I could sleep with you."

"Not a chance."

"It's ok," Noah said, glancing around. "I can sleep on the couch." His words carried very little conviction.

"Figure it out," Emily said, "and don't even think about getting a hotel. I'm making dinner. And I have wine. Noah if you'll come open it."

They got up and followed Emily to the kitchen where she had salad greens and pasta spread out on the large kitchen island.

She handed Noah the opener and the bottle of Pinot Noir.

Noah poured wine into three glasses. Savannah picked her glass up and gulped down several sips.

It was disconcerting being in her childhood home with her mother pushing her to spend the night with a man from her past whom she was barely reacquainted with.

For some odd reason, her mother seemed completely unsurprised to see them together. And determined to get them in bed together.

Perhaps she had fallen down a rabbit hole.

The irony of it all was, twenty years ago, there was no way in hell they would be allowed to sleep in the same room together in this house. Had that been her father's rule? Or had time merely mellowed her mother?

As her mother stirred her famous Italian sauce, Savannah washed and broke up lettuce and spinach and added it to a large salad bowl.

"What can I do to help?" Noah asked.

"You get a free pass this time," Emily said. "Next time you come over, you can help."

"Fair enough," he said, perching on a bar stool to watch them.

"Where do you live Noah?" her mother asked

Savannah cringed inwardly. She hadn't even bothered to ask Noah such a basic, albeit important question. Part of her hadn't wanted to know. As long as she didn't know such basic information, they still lived in a fairy tale world.

"I'm living in Ft Worth," he said.

"Near your family," she said.

"Actually, my father passed away a few years ago and my mother lives in an assisted living facility."

"I am so sorry to hear that," Emily said.

"Why didn't you tell me?" Savannah asked.

"It didn't come up yet. Actually I live there because I'm close to my daughter."

Savannah froze. Her hands chopping carrots. She looked up and met his gaze. "It didn't

come up yet?" she asked.

"I didn't want to freak you out."

"I'm not freaked out," she said. "You're a grown man. You should have children," she insisted, knowing her voice conveyed her surprise, nonetheless.

"Just one," he clarified.

She wiped her hair from her forehead with her wrist, continued to chop carrots, with a vengeance now.

Her college sweetheart had a daughter. The man she had thought, in her delusional world, was exactly the same man she had loved so many years ago, was now a man with a child.

Her brain attempted to integrate this new information. That Noah Worthington was a father. But her mind only wrapped around itself and ended up back where it started.

In a shock of disbelief. There was a time when she had thought they would have children together. And a picket fence. He had shattered that dream when he had disappeared.

Even now with their reconnection, that fantasy had been fanned back to life where it simmered in embers at the back of her mind.

But now…

"How old is she?" Emily asked, no doubt recognizing the look on her daughter's face.

"She'll be eighteen in a couple of months. She's a senior in high school."

Well, at least he had waited a little before getting someone else pregnant. Savannah kept her eyes down, picking up a stalk of celery and chopping it into a pulp.

The anger that welled into her was unexpected.

Anger wasn't one of the emotions she had ever connected with Noah.

But now… now that he was back in her life, her emotions had become more… well-rounded.

"I'm sorry," he said, softly.

I have no reason to be angry. It's not rational.

"Sorry for what?" She forced herself to look up, meet his gaze, forcing her lips to curve up at the corners in a semblance of a smile.

Emily had slipped out of the room, leaving them alone.

"I don't know," he said.

She forced herself to smile. "I'm just surprised, that's all. You must be very proud."

"I am," he beamed. "Would you like to see a picture?"

"Of course," she said.

"Here's her senior photo," he said, showing her a picture on his phone.

Noah's daughter was blonde. And beautiful. She had her daddy's eyes and someone else's bow shaped mouth.

"She's gorgeous," she said, and meant it. Of course, Noah would have a beautiful child.

"Guess the marriage was a little more than name only." She hated herself for saying it out loud. She just couldn't help herself.

"It was on our wedding night. It's the only time I ever

touched her. Every time I even looked at her, I felt like I was cheating on you."

Savannah digested that information. Allowed it to sink in. She hadn't been the only one in pain.

She inhaled deeply, steadied herself before looking into his eyes. Twenty years had passed between them. But there one thing she had to remember.

He was here now.

"I'll sleep on the couch," she said, dumping the celery and carrots into the salad bowl.

"Not a chance," he said.

"Ok, you can take the couch."

"Do you remember the last night we slept here?" he asked. "It was after midnight before I could sneak into your room."

"I was already asleep."

"Not for long," he reminded her.

She felt the heat creep up her cheeks. Being here reminded her just how much this man knew about her.

"I never told you," he said, picking up a carrot stick and munching on it. "I ran into your dad in the hallway."

Her eyes widened. "My dad saw you coming to my room?"

Noah nodded. "My hand was on the door knob."

Her dad had never said anything to her about seeing Noah that night. "What did he say?"

"He said 'good night Noah.'"

"Wow," she said. A whole host of emotions rushed through her.

She quickly tamped them back down and laughed. "I guess it wouldn't be all that strange, after all, for us to sleep in the same bed.

"Not for me," he said.

Before Savannah could process that comment, Emily came back into the kitchen and took plates from the cabinet. "Who's hungry?" she asked.

After dinner, the three of them went around and checked the door locks. After this morning's break in, Emily seemed to still be a little shaky.

Noah mostly followed along just in case he was needed.

"I'm gonna stay down here and read for a little while," he said, after Emily had gone up to bed.

"Sure," Savannah said. "There are blankets in the closet in case you get cold."

"I'm good," he said, opening his iPad.

Savannah went upstairs to her room, washed her face, and took a pair of sleep shorts and a t-shirt from the dresser. They had left their luggage in the car. Noah must have gone out to get a few things, but Savannah had basic clothes and toiletries here, at her mother's house.

She climbed into bed and listened to the familiar quietness of the house. The sounds were different from her house on Lake Martin. Here, the central air conditioning unit was just beneath her window. Subsequently, she didn't need the little white noise machine she used to lull herself to sleep at home. She blamed this air conditioner on her inability to sleep without a constant roar in the background.

The presence of other people in the house was different, she mused, from living alone. There was comfort in it.

She estimated that she spent about one fifth of her life in hotels. There was comfort in knowing that there were strangers sleeping next door, but it was a different kind of comfort.

It was unsettling that her mother's home had been broken into just earlier that day. She felt an uncertainty that resulted in knowing that they were vulnerable. Yet, with Noah downstairs, she felt safe.

Noah, the father.

Though she thought he should have told her about his daughter, she could understand why he didn't. He was divorced

– almost, and they were getting reacquainted. There were several things they hadn't discussed. Several things left over from years gone by. His daughter was just one of them.

Why he had left without a word was another. A big one. One she was beginning to understand.

But they seemed to have a tacit agreement that those things would be sorted out in good time. In the meantime, they were getting to know each other again. Getting to know the people they were now.

The same. Different.

She liked who Noah was now. He'd been cute when they were young, but now he was handsome. Successful. A pilot for a major airline.

She smiled as she considered that he had dropped everything to not only track her down, but also to stay with her. To show her the sights of New York. To get her home to resolve a family crisis.

He hadn't belittled the nature of the crisis as many others surely would have.

There was still a spark between them. Was that something that never completely died?

She was confused by the range of new emotions that he invoked in her.

She'd felt sad when he hadn't returned to Auburn all those years ago. But she'd quickly kicked that sadness into her studies.

Perhaps she hadn't dealt with his leaving. Perhaps she had unresolved issues.

Focusing on the moonlight shining through the bedroom widow, she attempted to quiet the thoughts rambling through her head.

Using the relaxation techniques she'd learned over the years, she drifted into sleep.

And in the darkness of night, with moonbeams shining

through her window, she dreamed that Noah snuggled next to her as she slept, holding her cradled with her back against his chest, his arms around her. His chin on the top of her head. The way they had slept so many nights so many years ago.

But when she woke, with the moonbeams replaced by the glow of the morning sun, she was alone in the bed. Only the faintest hint of masculinity lingered in the air and she dismissed it as her imagination.

It was most likely just the coffee and bacon she smelled drifting up from the kitchen.

NOAH LOVED TO COOK BREAKFAST. There was something about starting the day with a home-cooked meal that always put him in a good mood. He enjoyed the routine of it. The smell of it.

Emily had already been up when Noah went into the kitchen for morning coffee. There was a fresh pot next to the latte machine – no doubt there for Savannah's use.

He found a mug, left his coffee black. Searched out the Verismo pods needed to make Savannah's latte when she woke up. Considered taking coffee to her in bed, but decided that with her mother here, it was one gesture that should probably wait.

Instead he joined Emily in the sunroom. "Good morning," he said. "Am I interrupting?"

"Not at all," she said. "Please come on in. I spend more time alone than I care to admit."

"It's nice out here."

"I've got my plants and my birds out there. They'll be back." She nodded toward the bird feeders set up outside the window.

"Do you mind if I make breakfast?" he asked.

"Are you kidding? A man who can cook? And enjoys it. Does Savannah know how rare that is?"

"Savannah and I are slowly making our way back to being reacquainted."

"It shouldn't be all that hard."

"It takes a minute."

"Not much, I would think, after the way you two were attached at the hip."

"I apologize for the way that ended."

"I'm not the one you need to apologize to."

"You're absolutely right. I'm getting around to straightening all that out."

"It wasn't your choice, was it?"

"You're a wise woman, Mrs. Richards. You're right. There was a… problem with my father."

"I told her you had a good reason for what you did."

"Turns out the reason wasn't so good."

"I also told her you'd be back. I'm not sure that was the best thing to tell her. I think she waited for years for you."

"You can't know how much I regret that."

"Well… it seems I was right after all."

Noah laughed. "You were right after all."

They sat in silence for a few minutes. A couple of sparrows flitted around the bird feeder, but seemed more interested in each other than the bird seeds.

"How did you know?" he asked.

"I could say a mother knows these things, but honestly, it was just a lucky guess. And like I said, I had it off by too many years for it to count and for her own good."

"I hope to make that up to her."

"I would expect no less. I just have one thing to say."

"Sure," he said, steeling himself.

"Don't disappear on her again."

"Only if she runs me off."

"Ha. I hope you're not counting on that happening."

Noah drained his cup. "I think I'll get a refill and get started on breakfast. That is if you don't mind me in your kitchen."

"Absolutely I do not mind."

Emily's kitchen was organized to the hilt. It took him no time to find what he needed for a hearty breakfast.

He cracked eggs, flipped bacon, and grated some potatoes. It occurred to him that Savannah didn't eat this kind of breakfast. At least based on her menu choice of breakfast items yesterday.

Nonetheless, he made the things he liked to eat.

He did a double-take when he saw her standing in the door. She had on a white mid-calf length cotton robe that flowed around her, tied at the waist, fuzzy slippers on her feet, and her hair was tousled with sleep. He'd never seen her look so sexy.

"Good morning," he said, taking a step toward her to pull her into a hug. Her softness against him sent shock waves through his body. He had to remind himself that he had taken a personal vow to take it slow with her. To allow the trust to rebuild between them, at least on her part.

"Hi," she said, bending down to pick up Whiskers and held him close, petting his head. Whiskers meowed. "Meow. Meow. Me. Meow."

"The talking cat."

"See, I told you."

"I know you're not all that big on breakfast, but if you want to join me, I have enough."

Enough was an understatement. He'd counted on her eating with him. Somehow it had become very important that she be the one he could share his love of cooking breakfast with.

His ex had managed to always sleep through breakfast. The few times he had attempted to share, she had been on her way out. *Breakfast with the girls.* He always wondered why breakfast with her husband was never an answer.

But, then, neither one of them had ever been overly

enthusiastic about their arranged marriage. The fact that they had a daughter was a miracle in itself. If his child's eyes hadn't looked so much like his own, he would have wondered…

It had happened on the Celebrity cruise during the honeymoon. There was a martini bar right outside the main dining room. The bar was refrigerated and had a layer of ice on top. Kept the martinis deliciously cold. Martinis that were the best he had ever had before or since. Even extra olives, chilled to perfection, soaked in vermouth.

What happened after the martinis from heaven was a little hazy. He remembered rambling about how there should be benefits of holding the husband title. More benefits than what his father and his blackmail could provide.

He had no doubt she'd been willing. No haziness on that part. He wasn't the only one drinking martinis, after all. And it was their honeymoon. They'd spent the last two days pretending to like each other. *Fake it 'til you make it,* his mother had always said.

After the confined cruise, his society wife had managed to quickly find her way into Ft. Worth high society with frequent weekend trips home to California.

The trips had come to an abrupt halt, however, after the pregnancy. The math had been the easy part. Her obvious distaste for being confined to Ft. Worth was not.

He often wondered what her own father had threatened her with in order to make sure she married Noah. She never said and he had only asked once. Noah was a quick learner.

"You cook," Savannah said, gazing at him as though he was a unique specimen. Which, apparently he was. A man who could fly a plane, cook a meal, and look at her in a way that made her feel like she was the only woman on earth.

She sat at the little breakfast table and he set a plate of

scrambled eggs, bacon, hash browns, and toast in front of her. No jelly. Not her usual breakfast of granola and yogurt, nonetheless, one bite and she was hooked.

"You're a man of many talents," she said, between bites.

"I might be," he said, teasingly.

"You know," she said, holding her breath just a little, then plunging in. "I've kind of gotten used to you planning our days." She kept her eyes on her plate, nibbled a corner off the toast. She could so get used to this homemade breakfast thing, too.

He didn't respond. She actually wondered if he had left the room. When she looked up, he was grinning from ear to ear.

"I'm glad you said that," he said.

She smiled back. It was an involuntary reaction around him. "Why is that?" she asked.

"Because since I knew that you're still on vacation, I was toying around with a few ideas."

"Is that so?" She found that little smidge of cockiness irresistible. Always had.

"Yes," he said, sitting down to join her. "But first, I have to run a quick errand. Are you ok with staying here for a couple of hours?'

"Sure," she said. Cockiness and mysteriousness all swirled into one.

After breakfast, he rinsed and she placed the dishes in the dishwasher. "Have you seen my mom this morning?"

"She's in the sunroom."

"Still?"

He shrugged. "Maybe she was giving us a few minutes alone."

"Maybe," she said, though that truly did not sound like her mother. Her mother's philosophy was if someone came to visit, especially her daughter, they should have stayed home if they wanted alone time. But then, technically, with Noah here, it wasn't exactly alone time.

"I think I'll check on her, then get my shower."

"Sounds good. That'll give me more than enough time to get back."

He took her hand, kissed her knuckles, then pulled her into a tight bear hug. And held on like he never wanted to let go.

He pulled back enough to press a kiss against the corner of her mouth.

Then he was gone and she was left feeling a little bereft. A feeling she hadn't experienced since Noah had shown up at her hotel. Noah was going to be trouble, indeed.

On the way to check with her mother, she smiled to herself. In just a few short days, it seemed, she and Noah had once again become attached at the hip.

8

"Don't you have to be at work?" Savannah asked, cradling her Starbuck's coffee cup.

"I'm on vacation," Noah stretched out his long legs, watched her like a cat. "Don't you have meetings?"

"Not until Monday. I gave myself plenty of time to recover from the conference."

"Good idea."

"How much longer do you have off?"

"I haven't really decided yet," he said.

Savannah frowned. "That must be nice."

"Yeah," he said. "I kinda like it. It's giving me some ideas."

She looked askance at him. "What kind of ideas?"

"I'm thinking maybe I should quit and venture out on my own."

"That's kind of a giant leap, isn't it?"

"Now that I have my own plane, it isn't so much."

"Why now?"

"After my dad died, I decided to spend some of his money after all."

"Ironic."

He smiled. "It is ironic, I know."

"Has anyone ever told you that you have a… determined streak?"

"It may have come up." He sipped his coffee. Stared into space a moment. "So, if you could pick one place that you wanted to go, where would it be?"

"That's easy. I want to go to Venice."

"Ok," he laughed. "Let me rephrase the question. One place in the states."

"I don't know."

"Really? I could name five places right off."

"But you only said one. That's harder."

"Ok. Name five then."

"Denver. San Francisco. Salt Lake City, Las Vegas. Seattle."

He coughed, nearly spit out his coffee.

"That's interesting. You kind of like the west, I see."

"I've been to all these places for conferences. They were nice. Places I'd like to visit again."

"Oh. I see," his eyes took on a curious expression. "Name one place you'd like to go that you haven't been."

"That's harder. How would I know if I've never been there?"

That elicited an odd expression.

"Ok," she said. "I'll play along. I've always wanted to visit Mackinac Island."

"Where in the world is that?"

"Michigan."

He pulled out his iPad. Began typing. "It's a small airport," he said. "But the Mustang can handle it."

She chuckled. "The Mustang?"

He glanced at her, then back at his iPad. "The airplane."

She giggled a little, sipped her coffee. "You named your airplane."

"No, Silly," he said, turning his attention to her. "It's a Cessna Mustang. Cessna is the brand like Toyota. Mustang is the model name like a Camry."

"Oh," she said, trying to keep a straight face.

"It's like a Ford Mustang."

"Ok," she said, keeping an almost straight face. "I get it."

"Anyway," he said, shifting back to his iPad. "The weather looks good, but if it turns, we can land at Cheboygan and take a ferry."

She nodded, serious now. "No cars allowed on Mackinac."

"How do you even know about this island?"

"Seriously?"

"Yeah. An Alabama girl knowing about an island in north Michigan is a little… unusual."

"It's where Somewhere in Time was filmed."

He waited a beat. "I saw that movie. It was set there?"

"Yeah."

"I didn't know it was a real place. And if I remember correctly, he drove."

"He did drive, but that was just for the movie."

"Hmm. It says here there's a golf course just north of the airport. We can get a horse drawn carriage and stay at the Grand Hotel."

"Sounds nice."

"And you've never been there?"

"Never."

Five minutes later, he turned the screen so she could see.

He had pulled up a map from Birmingham to Mackinac Island with a line connecting them highlighted in magenta. There was a splash of green here and there and one splash of yellow, but nothing over their direct route.

"Good weather," he commented. "The green means light rain and the yellow means a little heavier rain."

"I'm well acquainted with the Weather Channel," she said, the amusement still playing about her lips.

According to the map, they could be there in two hours and ten minutes.

"Cool," she said. "It's a lot closer than I expected. Wouldn't you have to get approval to fly?"

"I would," he said, turning the iPad back so they could both see it. "We have to tell them when we're leaving." He looked at her questioningly.

"Let's say we wanted to leave now."

"Alright," he said. "We tell them there will be two souls on board." He clicked two.

"Souls! That sounds morbid. Almost like they're counting on a crash."

He grimaced. "Yeah. It's an archaic term, but it's still the way the FAA counts the number on board."

"Ok. Now what?"

"We're not far from the airport, but I'll give us an hour. So…" he checked his watch. "We should eat lunch first."

She nodded.

He typed in one o'clock. "That should give us plenty of time to eat lunch and get to the airport and get boarded." He hit enter.

"We're all set," he said.

"What else would you have to do?"

"We need to go eat and get to the airport."

"Now?"

"Sure. The flight plan is filed… and, your suitcase is packed from New York."

A little bubble of panic blocked her throat. She coughed.

"Our luggage is in the trunk of the car we borrowed from the airport," he reminded her.

"Well, yeah, but…" She did have her luggage packed. Hell,

she practically lived out of suitcase. "I have a suitcase full of heels, cocktail dresses, and business suits."

"The dress and heels will come in handy when we have dinner at the Grand Hotel."

"What about clothes? This is my only clean pair of jeans."

He clicked on his iPad again. "The hotel has a laundry and…" more clicking. "They have shops in town."

She took a deep, steading breath. Closed her eyes.

Noah put his hand on hers. "Savannah," he said. "No strings attached."

Savannah felt tears welling in her eyes. *No strings.*

She couldn't do no strings. Especially not with him. She shook her head, felt a tear slip down her cheek. She couldn't go down that route again.

"Hey," he said, "No, no."

He slid her against him, kissed the tear from her cheek, kissed her eyes, kissed her forehead. Tears started spilling from her eyes. Cradling the back of her head in his hands, he wiped them away, kissed the dampness of her cheeks. "I think I said the wrong thing," he said into her ear. "If you come with me, I insist on strings. Lots and lots of strings."

She laughed a watery laugh.

"I didn't mean to do that," she said. "I must look like a raccoon." She wiped at her eyes and came away with mascara on her fingertips.

"I like raccoons."

She laughed and looked into his eyes – his beautiful blue eyes. Eyes she knew so well. Eyes that now had little lines at the corners. Oh, so very sexy little lines. Her heart skittered the way it always did when she was this close to him.

"Give me a chance," he whispered.

With his words, she felt twenty years of heartbreak begin to melt away. Heartbreak she thought had been healed long ago.

. . .

Noah couldn't remember the last time he'd had so much fun. Flying was the one thing that had always brought him true happiness. Sitting here in his very own Mustang, the plane he'd been dreaming about owning for years was enough to make him ecstatic. But having Savannah sitting next to him, in the four-point safety harness, was enough to just about send him over the edge.

Did she have any idea the effect she had on him?

She wore jeans under what looked like a burgundy sweater dress with cute little motorcycle boots. Her eyes were bright as she watched everything he did. She had picked up the headset on her own so she could listen in to the traffic control chatter, even though she didn't need to. She could just as easily have stuck her head in a book and waited for him to get them to their destination.

But Savannah Richards was no spectator.

She was full of life and wanted to be a part of whatever she was doing.

While they had waited on their lunch at a local sandwich shop, they made a reservation online for the Grand Hotel. She hadn't objected when he'd reserved a two-bedroom suite for two nights. The anticipation of exploring the area with her was enough to have him pinching himself to make sure this wasn't another of his fantasies.

"That's us," she said, with her hand over the microphone, when their plane was cleared to taxi to the runway.

"I'm impressed," he said, after responding to the control tower. "By the way, you can talk," he told her. "I have you muted."

"Gee thanks."

He grinned. "I thought you might enjoy the freedom."

"I do." Nonetheless, she sat in silence as they taxied out to the runway. With Birmingham being a small airport, there was no wait.

He watched her clutch the edges of her seat as the plane went airborne. His favorite part of flying. Feeling nothing but air beneath him. For a moment in time, he was a bird.

As he checked controls, his mind went into autopilot.

How was this supposed to work? How long before he could begin thinking of her as his girlfriend again?

Ok. How long before he could begin calling her his girlfriend again? For twenty-one years, Savannah Richards had been his girlfriend.

She always was.

She always will be.

The thought came out of nowhere. Perhaps from the free air around them.

Oh, there was so much he had to make up for. The very fact that she had agreed to come with him meant that the stars had aligned, for once, in his favor.

He had been given a gift – a second chance and he would do everything in his power not to screw it up this time.

There was nothing anyone could say that could keep him from Savannah now.

With one exception.

Savannah.

He wouldn't have blamed her if she had never spoken to him again. But it was almost like they had picked up where they had left off.

He wondered how long he was supposed to wait before he kissed her again.

And again, the wind brought a swift answer to him.

She had settled into her seat now. It was hard to be excited for very long - when there was nothing to see but clouds and sky. And acres and acres of land beneath them. Besides, Savannah was a frequent flier, so that part wasn't new.

Once he had the plane leveled off, he set the autopilot control and, reaching out, took her hand. Their seats were close enough that if he leaned toward her and pulled her toward him just a little, he could put his arm around her.

She came willingly, tilting her head as though she thought he was going to tell her something.

He placed his hand under her chin and placed his lips lightly against hers.

They hit a pocket of air that had them reflexively clinging to each other.

All he could think was divine intervention.

His tongue lightly swept along her lower lip. He felt her shudder, whether from turbulence or his kiss, didn't really matter.

Everything he had pushed out of his memory. Everything that had faded from his mind about her, flooded back in a wave of sensations. Her feel. Her taste.

She dug her nails into his upper arms to bring him closer. There was no closer. Not with their harnesses in place and he wasn't about to release them with precious cargo in flight.

He deepened the kiss. His tongue swirled against hers. He wanted to taste everything. Feel everything all at once.

Don't rush. Take your time.

Forcing his sanity to return, he kissed her in a series of little short kisses. Little promises of more.

He pulled back, her eyes were closed, her lips parted.

He groaned. Kissed her again, lightly.

Willed her to open her eyes before he tossed caution to the wind and took her to the more comfortable back of the plane.

She blinked, opened her eyes. Smiled.

He scooted back in his seat. Checked his controls.

"We'll pick up there again soon," he said, his voice sounded gruff, even to his own ears.

Noah had a lot to do before landing. He checked the weather again. Spoke to the traffic controller in Minneapolis. Nothing coming in on Unicom. They were clear to land.

Curious about the island, he made a little loop around before lining up to the runway. The Grand Hotel, at least from the air, lived up to its name.

The landing took all his concentration. The short runway gave him no leeway for error.

After a smooth landing, he parked the plane and they climbed out. There was no car waiting for them here.

However...

Noah had called ahead, while Savannah had been in the restroom at the sandwich shop, and a horse and carriage waited for them, a driver dressed all in black standing at their beck and call.

"It's like a fairy tale," she said, turning to him, her face glowing.

Noah beamed. Pulled her against him and kissed her on the lips.

A fairy tale indeed.

SAVANNAH HUDDLED IN HER SWEATER, next to Noah. Her first purchase was definitely going to be a jacket.

The driver of the little carriage didn't seem to notice the cold.

"You two barely made it before the Grand Hotel closes next month," he said. "There are a few places open in winter, but it gets a little more difficult to get here. Especially after winter really gets going.

"Do people live here in the winter?" Noah asked.

"A few hearty souls. You won't catch me here though."

The ride to the hotel was elegant. The driver took them around so that they traveled along the tree lined road up to the hotel. When the Grand Hotel came into view, it nearly took her breath away. It was truly an American castle.

She smiled at Noah. It was hard to believe that just less than three hours ago, they had been sitting in Birmingham, Alabama. Not much longer than it would take her to drive from her home on Lake Martin to Atlanta for a day of shopping. Now here they were on the other side of the country in another world.

The driver stopped at the front of the hotel, and like royalty, they were greeted by the valet. The valet took their luggage and helped her from the carriage.

Noah took her hand as they went up the stairs, across the front porch, and through the lobby to the check in desk.

"Good afternoon," the clerk greeted them.

"We have a reservation for Worthington," Noah said.

"Ah. Welcome Mr. and Mrs. Worthington," the clerk said. "We have you in a lovely two-bedroom suite."

Savannah opened her mouth, but Noah just shrugged.

She didn't say anything. Didn't correct the clerk to tell her she wasn't Mrs. Worthington.

The clerk handed them keys – real keys, not key cards, and they followed the valet to the elevator and up to the fourth floor.

He opened the door, "Welcome to the newly renovated Cupola suite," he said.

"I tried to get the Somewhere in Time room," Noah said, "but it was already booked."

"No," Savannah said. "This is perfect." Everything was elegantly decorated. The walls were papered in a cheerful blue color, the drapes, the flowers. "It looks like a room for a princess."

After the valet left, Noah pulled her into a hug.

The clock on the wall chimed five times. "Hey," he said. "It's five o'clock."

"Time for a martini?" she asked.

He grinned. "You read my mind."

She laughed. Give me a minute to freshen up.

"Take your time."

Suitcase in hand, she paused, turned back to him. "Which one is mine?"

"You can have whichever one you want."

Savannah dragged her suitcase into the room to the right, which had two queen beds, dug her toiletry bag out of her suitcase, and went into the bathroom. She brushed her teeth, brushed her hair. It had been a long day, so there wasn't a lot she could do. She freshened her make-up, added some lip gloss.

Took a deep breath and stretched. Looked around. What were they going to do with all these beds?

At thirty-nine, she was not easily impressed.

And she knew better than to be swept off her feet.

This was a no strings trip.

It was important to keep her head out of the clouds. Noah may have been the one she'd always loved, but…

She ticked off the things to be wary of.

He was still married.

He had a daughter.

He had walked away from her once.

He had shattered her heart.

She shook her head. But she was here. Mentally rewrote her list.

He was almost divorced.

His daughter was an adult, so not a big issue.

He was here now.

There was still a place for him in her heart.

Much better. Putting a smile on her face, she went back to join him.

He was standing at the window so she could see his profile.

What she saw surprised her.

Instead of the carefree man he attempted to portray, in this unguarded moment, she saw pain.

What had caused him so much hurt?

She realized that whatever it was, she wanted to make it go away. Even if that meant setting aside the pain that he had caused her.

9

They sat next to each other at a little table in the huge lobby of the Grand Hotel, generously decorated with burgundy mums.

Noah drank a crown on the rocks and she sipped a pretty pink cosmopolitan. With olives.

"Tell me about your job," he said.

She shrugged. "It's really not all that interesting."

"Is that so. Well, let's see. You get to travel a lot."

"Travel is overrated."

"She said to the pilot."

Savannah laughed. "Right. No offense intended."

"None taken. You know a lot about prescription medications."

"I know a lot about psychotropic medications."

"Really? You specialize?"

"There are so many meds out there, you almost have to."

"So you only visit psychiatrists?"

"I prefer psychiatrists and medical psychologists, but Alabama doesn't recognize medical psychologists yet. I've visited a few in Louisiana and one in New Mexico. I'm a very strong advocate. They have their act together. I believe in medication. I have to. But I believe it works best with psychotherapy."

"I take it that doesn't go over all that well with general practitioners."

"I rarely even bother to mention psychotherapy to primary care providers. They don't have the time or energy to do more than prescribe a pill and send the patient on their way."

"That's unfortunate. I had a friend who tried the full range of SSRIs and finally landed on Lexapro. He pretty much had to figure out his own dosing regimen."

"Higher functioning patients can do that. But those are few and far between. Believe it or not, my most recommended SSRI is Prozac."

"Why Prozac? Isn't that the oldest one?"

"It has a built-in titration schedule. If the patient stops taking it all of a sudden, it stays in their system long enough to not cause any side effects from withdrawal."

"What about something like Xanax?"

"Ah. The benzos are wonder drugs. But docs don't like to prescribe them."

"I heard they're hard to get. What's the problem with them?"

"Unlike the SSRIs, they have to be titrated off. If not discontinued properly, seizures can occur. Also, in the elderly, they can cause dizziness and falling."

"They're ok in low doses, though, right?"

"I take Klonopin to help me sleep sometimes. Xanax works well, too, but it doesn't stay in the system long."

"You have to know all these drugs."

"I also know their systems like GABA. It's not required, really, that we know all that, but it seems to impress some of the docs and it's a good way to establish rapport. Besides, if I'm gonna be selling something, I want to know how it works."

"I can see why you're good at what you do."

"What makes you think I'm good at it?"

"You may recall that I heard you speak at a national conference."

She winced. "Right. You did, didn't you?"

"It's ok to be good at your job."

She swirled her drink, enjoyed the relaxed pace.

"Is it true?" he asked. What they say about drug reps?"

"What is it that they say?"

"That they'll do just about anything to get a doctor to agree to use their medications."

She scoffed. Refused to answer. "What about you? How good are you at your job?"

"I'm ok."

"Ok, my foot. You're with a major airline. Which I understand is hard to break into. And," she held up a finger. "You're good enough that you're thinking you can give that up and go out on your own doing contract work."

"Yeah," he said, rubbing his chin. "It's a hard decision with a daughter in college."

"It's weird to picture you as a dad."

"Hard to imagine, huh?"

"Not hard, just weird. In my head, you're still the college senior who wanted to grow up and be a pilot." She picked up a napkin. Held up the two sides. "Here's the Noah I knew," she said, "on this side and on this side is the Noah you are now." She put the two corners of the napkin together. "It's like all this," she swept a hand around the bottom of the napkin. "never happened. This is where all the mystery is."

"I'm still me," he said.

"Maybe. To some extent. But life has molded, changing you in perhaps small ways. It's like... Maybe you should get another drink."

He nodded. "Are you good?"

She placed her hand over the top of her glass. "Good."

He took his empty glass with him to the bar.

Savannah was enjoying her pretty pink cosmopolitan, but it was making her a little light headed. A little bold perhaps.

Or perhaps it was just sitting here in the Grand Hotel. From the movie she'd watched over and over as a teenager. And developed a huge crush on Christopher Reeve. She was actually here where the movie was filmed. It was almost like the movie had come to life.

She smiled, feeling like part of a private joke when Noah came back to the table.

"Are you having a good time."

"Absolutely."

"Good. Me too," he put his hand over hers. "What were you saying?"

For a moment, gazing into his clear blue eyes, she forgot what she was thinking, her thoughts scattered.

"It's like the neurons," she said, finding a thread of her previous thoughts.

"The neurons?"

He glanced at her drink. Frowned.

"When we have new experiences, we form new neuronal connections. Different experiences lead to different kinds of connections. These connections basically make us who we are. You've been married, you've had a baby, all sorts of things in the last twenty years. All those things have given you new emotions, new experiences. They've made you who you are."

She swirled her drink, took a swallow. He was watching her closely.

"Are you nervous?" he asked.

"Me? No. Why would I be nervous?"

"I don't know. But you've only had about a fourth of that drink and I've seen you be unaffected after drinking a whole lot more." He slid the drink over, sniffed it, slid it back.

"Is my drink ok?" she asked, with a mischievous smile.

"There's nothing wrong with your drink."

"Good. Because I'm enjoying it."

"I haven't seen you like this since…"

"Since when?"

"Never mind," he said, "There are probably some things we need to talk about."

"Oh no," she said, leaning forward. "Listen. I understand the whole concept of being in the moment. I'm into the moment. Let's not look into the past and let's not look forward tonight."

"Ok," he said. "I thought you wanted to look into the napkin."

"I changed my mind."

He ran his hand through his hair. "Sure."

"Look where we are," she said, sweeping her hand upwards. "Did you have any idea that we'd be thousands of miles away from home tonight on this beautiful, historic island?"

"No, but technically we were thousands of miles away from home two nights ago, too, when we were in New York."

"And that was lovely. But it was planned."

"Planned for you, perhaps."

"Ah ha."

"Ah ha what?

"No, we're not talking about that tonight."

His eyes narrowed and she smiled.

"Tonight we're on the same page. We're doing something together that neither one of us planned."

"You're right," he conceded. "So what do you want to do tomorrow?"

"I just want to be with you," she said. Then smiled broadly. "We can do whatever we want because neither one of us has any expectations from the other."

. . .

NOAH DOWNED the rest of his drink.

Savannah knew exactly what she was doing.

She was getting him off-guard. He wasn't sure yet, but he knew she wasn't intoxicated and she wasn't blonde. However, at the moment, she could easily have passed for either.

He figured she wanted to talk about their past. Wanted to so bad she could taste it. She was toying with him. Making him think she didn't. Making him think she was not concerned with their future. He was pretty sure she was very concerned with their future.

Her being here was quite a leap of faith. Savannah Richards didn't do anything lightly. And she was not spontaneous. She was a planner. He knew that if he checked the electronic calendar on her phone, she would have meetings scheduled and trips laid out for the next few weeks, conferences planned for the next year, and who knew what else.

This lack of structure, this ambiguity was enough to drive her over the edge. She did nothing without purpose, but she would deny it. She believed she was spontaneous.

At least, he reminded himself, that was the Savannah he had known before. Perhaps it would be interesting to test his theory. To see if that had changed.

"When's the last time you had free time like this to do whatever you wanted?"

She pursed her lips. "It's been a little while. Why?'

"Just curious. I feel lucky that you were able to get away with me."

"I didn't plan on it," she said.

"I know. That's why I feel lucky. When is your next conference?"

"There's a three day at New Year's."

"You have a conference on New Year's?" He ignored the flash of disappointment.

"Technically, it doesn't start until the day after New Year's, but I usually go early. They always have some sort of New Year's Eve party."

It was worse than he thought. Even her New Year's Eves were planned months in advance.

"How often do you see your daughter?"

"At least once a week."

He also knew that she did not want to talk about his daughter. But she wouldn't be able to resist it. His daughter represented everything she missed out on with him.

But she didn't realize yet that it didn't have to be that way.

"What about you?" he asked. "No children?"

She shook her head. Gave him the canned response. "My lifestyle didn't really allow for it. I always thought there would be time someday."

"So you never got around to it," he said.

"Exactly."

"Savannah." He held her gaze. "You always told me you wanted two kids and a cat. You said you wanted everything normal in life."

"I do want everything normal in life."

"You say that, but you don't have those two kids. You don't even have the cat."

"I could have a cat."

"Your mother has a cat. You don't. You're gone too much and you wouldn't do that to a pet."

"You're analyzing me now."

He laughed. "I'm a pilot. I don't analyze people. You do."

"I push medications. I don't analyze."

"How many conferences have you attended on psychology? To learn how to analyze people and push their buttons to make them want to choose your drugs over someone else's? Why do you think you're so good at your job?"

"I'm good at my job because I work hard."

"Yes, you do. And you make time for things that are important to you."

He'd pushed her too far. He could see it in her face. Oh no! *Please don't cry again.*

She recovered quickly, though. "When I meet the right person, I'll think about having a baby."

"Aren't you worried about the ticking biological clock?"

"I'm only thirty-nine. I've got another good five to ten years before I have to worry about that."

"It takes a minute to meet the right person and get all that in place."

There was that look again. That deer in the headlights look.

"I'd like another drink," she said. "Would you get me a martini with extra olives?" She held out her glass with the unfinished cosmopolitan.

Noah took the glass and went back to the bar. He should feel pleased that he'd turned the tables on her and now she was the one unsettled instead of him.

But he didn't. He, too, wanted to talk about their past. He wanted to explain everything. Tell her everything about his life for the last twenty years. But he knew it would be painful for her to hear. He would have to continue to tell her little pieces at the time.

He also wanted to talk about the future. He wanted to be on her daily day planner. But before he could get to the future, he had to right the past.

He took the martini from the bartender, tasted it. It wasn't bad. Not too strong. He wanted Savannah clear-headed. He wanted her to make good decisions where he was concerned. He didn't want her judgment clouded with alcohol.

Well, maybe just a little.

The lobby was filling up now. They weren't the only people staying here after all. Dinner would be served soon. Tomorrow they would go downtown and look around at the shops. They might even walk around the beach.

A few feet from their table, he froze.

She wasn't there.

In fact, there was no sign of her. Her handbag was gone, too. He looked around frantically. He'd brought her all the way to Michigan only to have her snatched?

His heart pounded in his chest. Had she left him? Had he pushed her too far after all?

Setting the drink on the table, he had the most bizarre sensation that she had been no more than a fantasy. He traveled alone so much, that perhaps it had gotten to him. Now he was imagining conversations with people.

He stood at the table, frozen. Not sure whether to get himself home and admitted to a psych ward or to turn this island upside down in a frantic search for Savannah.

He turned, then, and saw her walking toward him. Relief flooded through him. When she reached him, he hugged her tightly.

"You missed me?" she asked.

"I was trying to figure out what I was going to tell your mother about your kidnapping."She laughed. "You make it sound like having your dates kidnapped is a common occurrence."

"I don't date," he said.

"What do you mean?"

"You're the only girl I've ever dated."

AN ELDERLY MAN in a dark gray suit came around to each table, one by one to let them know that dinner was being served in the main dining room. "The meal is included with your stay, but you have to put on a tie, sir and, miss, I'm sorry, but no denim allowed."

"That's not a problem," she said. She had a suitcase full of formal attire. And knew that Noah had a tux with him. After all, they hadn't changed out their clothing after returning from New York.

"Very good," the man said, "we look forward to seeing you there."

"What do you think?" he asked. "Should we go or look for someplace less formal?"

"I think I'd rather put on a dress than venture out tonight. How about you?"

"Sounds good. Want to finish your drink first?"

"Nope. I'm good."

It was a bit of a walk back up to the room. Once inside, they went into their respective rooms and dressed for dinner.

Savannah put on her red high low dress and black heels. Her floor length gown seemed a bit formal for the occasion. She felt a bit rushed as she ran a brush through her hair and reapplied lip gloss.

They met back in the parlor and didn't waste any time for the hike back down to the dining room.

The dining room was surprisingly crowded. The required formal attire gave it a different atmosphere than it had earlier. It looked less touristy now and more formal and historic. They were seated at a table with an excellent view of the water – just as the sun was setting.

Noah ordered a smoked salmon roulade for an appetizer and a bottle of pinot noir.

Savannah wanted to get back to their earlier conversation. At the moment, however, he seemed to be intent on distracting her with small talk.

"Did you know that the hotel has three hundred ninety rooms and no two are exactly the same?"

"I did not. That's pretty amazing."

"And," he continued. "The front porch is the longest in the world."

"Did you know that there's a Somewhere in Time fan club that meets next week?"

"That's unfortunate. We just missed it."

"It's ok. I think it would be distracting."

"I thought that's something you would enjoy."

"Maybe," she said, "I'm in more of a low-key mood right now."

The server appeared to take their order. She ordered the roasted eggplant casserole and he ordered the whitefish.

"We have to order one those Grand Pecan Balls for dessert. It's their most famous dessert."

"I don't suppose they have a treadmill."

"With all the bicycling, walking, and such on the island, I doubt you'll need it."

"I guess I can count that as cardio."

"I admire your health consciousness," he said.

"With everything I know about biology, it's hard not to take exercise seriously."

"I need to follow your example."

"I don't mind the company."

The server brought their bottle of wine, uncorked it, and poured a taste in Savannah's glass. She sipped. "Wow. This is really good wine."

"Only the best, Miss. Is this your first time to the Grand?"

"It is," she said, glancing at Noah. "We're quite impressed."

"Thank you miss," he said. "I hope you enjoy your stay."

He filled their glasses, wiped the bottle with a white cloth, and went to check on their appetizer.

"We are impressed, aren't we?" she asked, turning back to Noah.

"We are ecstatic."

She smiled, glanced around before turning her gaze back to

Noah. "I know we haven't had a chance to explore the island yet, but based on your first impression, which do you prefer, New York or Mackinac?"

"That's like asking me if I like apples or oranges. They're both great, and I couldn't possibly choose one over the other."

"Aw. That's a cop out and you know it."

"I know one thing."

"What's that?"

"I like you."

She paused, her glass halfway to her lips.

"I certainly hope so since you brought me up here to the top of the world."

He laughed. "It seems more like you brought me."

She smiled. Either way. "I hadn't planned on taking a vacation right now."

"Unplanned vacations are the very best kind."

"I had no idea."

The server brought their appetizer and Noah tasted it first. "Oh wow. You've got to try this."

She took a bite of the salmon with dill cream and caviar. "This is…hmm. Unlike anything I've had before." She took another bite.

"You like it?"

"It's like heaven."

Noah beamed as though he had made it himself.

"You've had this before," she said.

"I've actually made this before."

"You? No way."

"I did. I took a cooking class last year and this is one of the things we made. You take some cream cheese and some dill and roll it up like a jelly roll."

This was a Noah she did not know. And hadn't expected. "Why did you do that?" Was all she could think to ask.

"I knew I was getting divorced and it just seemed like something interesting to do"

She couldn't help the accusing tone that came next. "You wanted to attract women."

"You're attracted to men who can make salmon roulade?"

"That would be strange," she said.

"Perhaps, but you avoided the question."

"I do like a man who can cook and will cook," she took another bite of salmon. "There is huge difference in the two."

"Sounds like you're speaking from experience."

"I might be."

"Well, in my house, if there was cooking to be done." He stopped himself in mid-sentence. Appeared to regroup. "Let's just say that in my previous relationship, I'm the one who of us who cooked."

"You just kept something from me," she said.

He sat back, sipped his drink. "Very perceptive, my dear."

"I think that's the problem," she said. "You've been holding out on me for a while… about twenty-one years."

"Why would you think that?"

"At the time I didn't notice, but in retrospect, you knew everything about me and my family, but I knew nothing about where you came from. I met your parents once. And they were not ordinary parents."

"I'm not sure that's a compliment."

"Noah," she said, setting down her fork. Leaning forward. "I know now why you kept me from your family."

He shook his head, imperceptibly.

The sounds of live musicians drifted from the other end of the dining hall.

"Looks like they have live music," Savannah pointed out.

"No. No. Don't change the subject. Why did I keep you from my unordinary family?"

"I was an ordinary girl and your father was a tycoon."

"What makes you say something like that?"

Savannah knew she was on the right track by the way his eyes widened. "He had the tycoon look."

"I didn't realize tycoons had a look," he glanced around the dining area. "Are any of these men tycoons?"

"No," she said. "Besides the tycoon look, you obviously inherited enough money to use *some* of it to buy yourself an airplane. I can add, Noah."

The server, dressed in black tie, brought a tray to their table, two plates, covered with silver domes. He uncovered each one to serve their food. Heat from the white plates, elegantly presented, wafted between them.

Noah appeared relieved to have a moment to collect his thoughts.

"I apologize, Noah. I shouldn't have said anything."

"It's ok," he said, tasting his fish. "This is awesome fish!"

Savannah tasted her own food. It was, indeed, tasty.

"You're right," Noah said. "My father was wealthy."

"Noah..."

"No. I always tried to keep that from you. I wanted to be normal. Regular. In college. Even the boat. It was my boat. But I didn't want you to see me that way."

"Noah," she breathed. "You should have known. It wouldn't have changed anything. I loved you from the very beginning."

"I didn't know that then. I needed to know that it wasn't my money you were after."

Savannah lowered her lashes and set her fork down. Everything she knew about Noah shifted into place. Everything she had suspected after he went away. Now that she knew, she expected it to matter. But it didn't.

He was still Noah.

They finished their food in silence. Savannah ate a few more bites, but she had lost her appetite.

By the time the server removed their plates, one of the

couples was dancing a few yards away. They watched as another couple joined them.

Suddenly, Noah stood, went around the table and stood in front of her and held out his hand. "Dance with me, Savannah," he said.

She shook her head.

"Come on. Don't make me look foolish."

She put her hand in his and allowed him to lead her to the dance floor. He put one hand on her waist and, holding her other hand, led her into a waltz.

Another one of Noah's secret talents.

"I went to a boarding school," he said, when she looked at him questioningly.

"I have no idea how to do this," she said.

"Just follow my lead," he said, sending her into a twirl.

Noah was indeed a good dancer. So much so, that they drew a bit of an audience. After the first dance, other couples joined them until the area around them was crowded.

Then the music slowed and he pulled her to him. Put his arms around her waist. Her hands wrapped around his neck and she laid her cheek against his chest.

Safe.

Cherished.

Those were the two emotions that flooded her senses.

Noah.

She sighed.

Nothing in her life had made as much sense before or after him.

The years faded. Folded in until, although it may still exist, the time that had elapsed no longer mattered.

She was in Noah's arms. The one place she had always belonged.

. . .

Noah swayed with Savannah in his arms. How had he let her go so long ago?

There must be a God, indeed, for him to have not only found her, but to have the honor of her allowing him back into his life.

A second chance.

He'd been granted a second chance. And he would not. Could not. Mess it up this time.

He slipped a hand up to her chin, gently tilted her face up. Her eyes were closed. He stroked her cheek, the edge of her lips. Her lips quivered ever so slightly.

He groaned.

Pressed his lips against hers.

She melted against him.

A room.

He needed to get her to their room.

He reached down. Picked her up.

Her eyes flew open.

He carried her back to their table. Slid her down against him.

His body still pressed against hers, he swept her hair back and tucked it behind her ears. "What am I going to do with you, Savannah Skye?" he asked, his voice next to her ear.

"Is it so difficult to figure out?" she asked, her voice quivering.

"Turns out I'm a little slow sometimes."

He felt her laugh against him.

"You're the smartest man I know."

"Spoken by the girl who cavorts with doctors."

"I wasn't thinking of them."

"You really know how to stroke a man's ego," he said.

"I think I had too much to drink," she said.

He glanced toward the table at the glass of wine she'd barely touched.

"You didn't even have half a glass."

"Must be the elevation," she said.

"Must be," he agreed, releasing her enough to pick up her handbag, but still steadying her with his other arm. "How about we get out of here?"

"I thought you'd never ask."

He took her hand and after a chaste kiss on the forehead, led her toward the elevators.

They walked in comfortable silence, only the sound her heels echoing softly down the long hallway.

Noah wanted more than the chaste kisses on the cheek. He wanted more than kisses while locked in a four-point shoulder harness.

But he also wanted more than passion in the sheets.

He wanted everything. And the heat was still there between them. Perhaps even more so. They were stoking a fire than had been smoldering for twenty years.

But most of all, he wanted her heart back. Once and for all.

They had waited this long. There was no reason not to wait a little longer before rushing into consummating their relationship.

"I need a minute," Savannah said, once they were in the room.

She went into her part of the suite and Noah, knowing it would be more than a minute, went to his room and changed into a pair of warm sweatpants and a t-shirt. Washed his face and brushed his teeth.

He went back to the common area and stretched out on the sofa to wait.

A few minutes later, Savannah joined him, her face scrubbed free of make-up, she also wore a t-shirt and long pajama pants.

"It's cold," she said, as he gathered her into his arms on the sofa.

"I'll keep you warm," he said.

"Ok," she said, snuggling against him. He gently rubbed her back, making little circles at the back of neck.

She grew still against him. He shifted slightly. Her eyes were closed and her lips slightly parted.

She'd fallen asleep.

He gathered her into his arms and carried her to her bed, tucked her beneath the comforter.

He watched her sleep for a few minutes.

Then went to the sofa, stretched out his long legs, and pulled a fleece throw up to his chin. Tucking his arms behind his head, he watched Savannah's door.

Guarding her perhaps.

Definitely struggling with the magnetic pull to go to her.

10

Savannah woke early the next morning. Disoriented. Despite her frequent hotel stays.

She checked her phone. It was only five thirty.

Then she realized why she was disoriented. It was pitch black in the room. Typically, she liked to keep the curtains open whether in a hotel or in her second story bedroom at home.

She climbed out of bed and opened the curtains. No street lights.

She wandered into the living room.

Noah was curled up on the sofa beneath a blanket.

He had his own room.

She walked over, peeked inside. His bed was still made. His suitcase stood next to it. Unpacked.

Perplexed, she went back to the living area and sat in the chair next to the sofa.

Wondered if the hotel did room service.

After about three minutes, she went to her room and dug into her own suitcase for her workout clothes. She had a pair of tights which, according to her phone, should be weather appropriate. She tied her sneakers, tucked her phone and room key into a pocket on her tights and headed outside.

It was early and she appeared to be about the only one up and about.

Stepping outside into the chilly air, she skipped her warm up and started jogging down the main road. It felt good to stretch her legs. To have a few minutes to herself when she didn't have to think.

Her mind could just wander down its own path with no direction.

Naturally, it wandered to Noah.

Why on earth had he slept on the sofa when he had a perfectly good bed?

She didn't remember how she had ended up in her bed last night. But she did remember being so incredibly sleepy.

Her path took her downtown next to the waterfront. There were a few people about, mostly headed to work, it seemed.

She spotted a Starbuck's and was instantly ecstatic. Going inside, she was the only customer.

She ordered a vanilla latte, paid with her phone app and strolled back outside. Walking now, she studied the quaint little town. Mostly tourist shops and restaurants.

It was perfect.

She found a bench on a path next to the beach and sat watching the sun come up.

A young couple, walked past, hand in hand, and Savannah decided she should get back to Noah before he got up and discovered her missing.

She finished her coffee as she walked back through town. At the edge of town, she began jogging again. The warmth of the sun, the jog, and the hot coffee had her perspiring a bit.

She went back through the lobby, up the elevator, and down the long hall to their room.

Used her key and stepped into the room.

Noah was there, holding his phone with one hand, the other hand pressed against the side of his head. He turned, saw her. "She's here. Thank God. I'm sorry I bothered you. Yes. Thank you."

Noah stared blankly at her.

"What's going on?" She asked, taking her phone out of her pocket.

"Savannah." He looked a little pale.

"What?"

"Where have you been?"

"I went for a jog," she picked up a bottle of water, opened it, and drank about half of it.

"A jog."

"The town is really pretty," she said. "And they have a Starbucks."

"I was in the process of reporting you missing."

"Missing?"

"You weren't here."

Oh crap. "I'm sorry."

"Hand me your phone," he said.

She handed him her phone.

He clicked, handed it back. "You have to unlock it."

She used her fingerprint to unlock it, handed it back. She drank more water. Watched him warily. "What are you doing?"

He was typing into her phone. "Here," he said, when his own phone started to ring, handing her back her phone.

He clicked the keys on his own phone. "Now I can call you when you're lost."

"I wasn't lost," she said, but knew exactly what he meant. "I'm sorry," she said again.

"You really are used to being alone."

She shrugged. He appeared to be calming.

"So, where's my coffee?"

Her eyes widened. She should have brought him coffee. "It would have been cold by the time I got back."

"I'm only kidding. It would be hard to jog with coffee in your hand."

"Why did you sleep on the sofa?"

He picked up the blanket. Folded it. "I fell asleep," he said.

She waited for him to expound on his answer, but instead, he went toward his bedroom. "I'm going to take a shower," he said.

"Good idea," she said. "Me, too." But she didn't think he heard her.

Letting the hot water run over her head, Savannah tried to sort out what had just happened.

She'd been awake and restless. So she'd gone jogging. It wasn't like there was a treadmill in the room.

And, she admitted, she had taken time at the Starbucks and watching the sun come up. She'd been gone, what? A little over an hour. She hadn't kept track.

She really hadn't expected him to even know that she was out. Had he gone into her room?

If they had true separate rooms, instead of a suite, he certainly wouldn't have known.

They had, it seemed, progressed a bit in their relationship.

She got out of the shower and put the same jeans back on that she had worn yesterday. She could not however, bring herself to wear the same sweater. Consequently, she wore a silk blouse. She never wore the same clothes two days in a row. But she didn't want to wear a dress or slacks.

Noah had promised that there would be shops.

Unfortunately, she wasn't sure he was talking to her now.

She put on her make-up and dried her hair.

Noah was waiting for her when she went back into the living area.

"Ready for breakfast?" he asked.

"Sure."

He took her hand and together they went into the hallway toward the elevator.

"I'm sorry I overreacted," he said.

"I'm sorry I left without telling you. You're right. I have spent too much time alone."

"I guess we both have some adjustments to make," he said, with a smile.

"Yes, I suppose we do," she returned his smile. His comment gave her hope that he was thinking forward to the future.

They rode in a horse drawn carriage downtown, then Savannah had her second, albeit smaller cup of coffee. She didn't have the heart to tell him she'd already been to Starbucks.

She bought a gray sweatshirt, one that zipped and wore it out of the store.

They had an early lunch and watched the ferry bring in the tourists for the day. Some of them had luggage with them.

"Flying is definitely the way to get here," Savannah commented.

"I'm glad you're finally on board with the whole flying thing."

"I've always been on board. But after this past week, I'm not sure I'll ever be the same."

Her comment elicited a smug look which Savannah found amusing. Noah was so easily complimented. As long as it was about flying.

After lunch, they rented bicycles for the rest of the day and started their trek around the island. It wasn't crowded. They only saw a few others out walking and one other man riding.

About halfway around, they stopped to take a break and admire the view.

"I'm glad you picked this place," Noah said. "There are so

many beautiful places to see in this country. I'd like to see them all."

"It would take a lifetime," Savannah said. "How would you even find all the places to see?"

"We could go state by state. Research it."

"You sound almost serious. What would you do? One state every year?"

"We'd have to do more than that. I guess it would depend on the state. And how much time we had to devote to it."

Savannah leaned back and savored the sun shining on her face. They had settled into their old companionship. Savannah was reminded that she'd had no other relationship like the one she'd had with Noah. Had he? Had he had other relationships like this?

He had definitely set the bar for her early.

"There's something you should know about me," she said.

He turned his attention to her. "I'm listening."

"Just before you start planning these trips, you should know that I'm not really an outdoor kind of girl."

"Is that so? You seem to be riding that bicycle ok."

"Yeah. But I'm not into the whole camping thing. I prefer to sleep in a warm bed. With room service."

"No need to worry, ma chérie, we are of like mind when it comes to that."

She smiled at the endearment. And turned her gaze to meet his. "There's a chill in the air," she said.

He pulled out his phone. "I should check the weather."

"Now?"

"Unfortunately, our return flight home depends on the weather."

"Let's just stay here."

"Don't tempt me," he said.

After an afternoon of bicycling, Savannah was exhausted.

She'd used muscles she didn't know she had. She made a mental note to add cycling into her workout routine.

Noah determined that they should leave early the next morning due to an impending cold front. Savannah was disappointed. There was so much more on the island that she wanted to see. Noah was opening up worlds she didn't even know existed.

They had a quiet dinner at the hotel, then rented a movie in their room. Noah didn't drink, but Savannah had a glass of wine. "Twelve hours bottle to throttle," he'd said. Apparently, that rule also applied to sleep. At nine o'clock he announced that he was going to sleep – in his bed.

"I'm glad you're going to get some use out of your bed," Savannah commented.

"Ha. So, you'll be ready by seven?"

"I'd prefer to stay here for a week," she said.

"As would I," Noah agreed, "instead, we'll put this on our list of places to visit again."

"Deal," she said, as he kissed her good night.

And, with his kisses, he was bringing to life fantasies that she had given up on years ago.

It seemed he would only be getting eleven hours of sleep, she mused, as they settled into the kiss.

11

Noah landed the plane and taxied down the runway. Glancing at his watch, he knew he would be early for his three o'clock meeting.

He took a deep breath and forced himself to relax. There was a lot riding on the meeting, yet, no matter how it went, he knew he had more options.

Two hours later, Noah stepped out of the bank building and went straight to his BMW SUV. The meeting had gone well.

In less than a month, he would begin his transition process toward retiring from the airline and doing his own contract work. The older pilot, Sam Allen was ready to give up his business. He was ready to spend his days on the beach with the love of his life.

Noah loved Sam's story. It reminded him a lot of himself and Savannah.

Sam had only been married for ten years, but those ten years had been a long time coming. He and his wife had gone to high school together, but they hadn't gotten to know each other until twenty –five years later after they had run into each other in their hometown. Neither one of them had lived there since high school, so it was rather happenstance that they had even recognized each other. They had both been married at the time, but had stayed in touch as friends. Then, ten years later, they had met again, this time he was divorced, but she was still married. They had begun talking on the phone anyway. As friends. After her husband died from heart disease, they had gone on their first date. They were married a week later.

Sam knew that had created quite the gossip flurry, but neither he nor his wife cared. Now that they were in their sixties, they found the whole thing amusing. They just wanted to live out their days on the beach, holding hands, and drinking Piña coladas.

Sam had built up quite the business. So much so that he had three younger pilots flying for him.

Unfortunately, Sam had no children, so there was no one to pass the business along to. Sam and Noah had met years ago at a week-long training for certification for flying the Learjet, and had become friends immediately.

They'd stayed in touch and Sam had been telling Noah for years that he should come work for him.

Noah had picked up the phone the day after he returned from Mackinac and set up the meeting with Sam to work out the details.

Now that Sam was retiring, Noah was getting more than he had bargained for. He was getting Sam's business. That meant he could take the jobs he wanted and let the younger guys have the other ones. Noah liked the idea of having that kind of freedom mixed with security.

And the great thing about being a pilot was he could work from anywhere.

He was meeting Sam and his wife, Beth, at a restaurant in Dallas. Noah didn't mind. It was on his way home. Sam had to run home and pick up his wife, so Noah would have a few minutes to have a drink at the restaurant bar and unwind.

He chose a seat toward the back, at the bar, away from the noise, ordered a crown on the rocks, and opened his iPad.

He had an email from Claire, his soon to be ex-wife.

Hi Noah,

I hope you're doing well. It seems like we haven't spoken in forever. I met with the attorney today and we have court day for December 16. The week before Christmas! I got a sick feeling just thinking about it. I don't know why. Lol. It's not like we had the best relationship. And I know I was one to initiate the divorce. At least I think I was. I think you smiled quite a bit during the whole packing process.

Anyway, I thought that if you were having second thoughts, this might be a good time to talk about it.

Love ya,

Claire

Noah stared at the email. Where was the Claire he had been married to?

Had she ever told him she loved him?

For his daughter's sake, sure, but truly of her own volition? He was certain she hadn't. They had only been intimate that one time on their honeymoon on the cruise.

He had been fairly certain she was only biding her time, based on the prenuptial agreement.

The server brought his drink. He sipped. Considered. What was her angle? She was after something, he had no doubt. Perhaps their daughter had been looking over her shoulder. Whatever it was, he couldn't possibly imagine it being anything sincere. Or good.

It didn't matter anyway. There was no way this side of hell that he was going to rethink this divorce. In fact, December 16 was much farther off than he would prefer.

"Mind if I sit here?" The decidedly female voice interrupted his contemplation.

"Sure," he said, absently, barely glancing toward the blonde in the sleek red dress. He returned to his iPad. No other emails. He reminded himself that Savannah didn't have his email address.

She did have his phone number though. He checked his phone. No text messages.

It had been five days since he'd dropped her off at her home. He hadn't gone inside. He'd wanted to give her some space. He didn't want to make too many assumptions. He knew he couldn't expect to just waltz back into her life and upend everything. She was obviously busy and successful.

She wasn't however, seeing anyone, which he found comforting. He liked knowing she was out there. Busy. Perhaps thinking of him.

Just a little.

"Busy day?" the woman asked.

Jarred out his thoughts again, Noah looked up to the woman sitting on the bar stool next to him. The bar wasn't crowded. There were about a dozen other places she could have sat.

"I'm Abigail," she said, holding out her hand.

"Noah," he said, automatically shaking her hand.

He refocused on his iPad. Not seeing it now.

"Can I buy you a refill?" she asked, indicating his drink.

When it rained, it poured.

"No, I'm good."

"No, really… Bartender," She gestured for the bartender. "I'll buy him another of what he's having."

Noah shook his head, but the bartender was already off to fetch his drink. Noah knew how this game played out. He'd end up buying the drinks. If she had her way, they'd end up in a room together.

But that wasn't going to happen. Noah was no saint. He'd done two one-night stands years ago. Each time, he woke up feeling unfulfilled.

Besides, all he could think about was Savannah. Then and now.

Perhaps he should call her tonight. But he was more of a show up out of the blue kind of guy. Maybe he liked the effect it had or maybe he just wasn't sure what he should say to her.

Perhaps he should at least send her a text.

He typed *Hi. It's Noah. How's your week?*

Abigail's drink arrived.

"No thanks," Noah said. "I'm meeting someone." He hit delete.

"Alright," she said, "But I don't think she's coming."

Noah stared at his phone. Still no text from Savannah. He'd had to text her a couple of times while they were at Mackinac and she had responded immediately. He knew she had his number because he had put it there himself.

"No," Noah said, not even looking at her as he stood up and started toward the door. He'd wait for Sam outside if he had to.

Sam and his wife arrived at the restaurant a few minutes later. Beth was an elegant woman, charming, always wearing a smile on her face. She hugged Noah in greeting.

After they were seated, Sam ordered a bottle of champagne. Noah was reminded of Savannah and her love of mimosas. He suddenly wanted her there with him. Badly. She should be here.

She would enjoy Beth and Sam and they would enjoy her company. His idea to surprise her with the news of the deal he was making suddenly felt like not such a good idea. It would have been better to involve her in the process.

He took out his phone, stared at the offending blank screen.

It was Friday night. What was she doing?

Was she out?

Savannah had told him she didn't do the whole going out with girlfriends thing. She could be with her mother or her sister.

Or she could be on a date.

"Is something wrong, Dear?" Beth asked.

"No, not at all," Noah said, and put his phone away. He would deal with this later.

Over appetizers, Noah asked Beth to tell him how she and Sam got together. He had heard Sam's version. He wanted to hear hers.

"Oh, in high school, he didn't even know I existed. Then we kept running into each other over the years."

"I knew you existed," Sam protested.

"It's alright," she said. "I had a huge crush on the football captain."

"You never told me that."

"A girl has to have a little mystery," she said, with a bright smile at Noah. "Right, Noah?"

"Most women do," he said.

"We have to keep you interested somehow," she told her husband.

Sam took her hand, kissed her knuckles.

Noah looked away and his gaze landed on Abigail. She had taken a table just out of earshot. She smiled broadly at Noah.

He scowled.

And had a flash of boiling bunnies.

"Noah, do you know that woman?" Beth asked.

"I met her at the bar before you came in," he said.

"Do you want to invite her over?" Beth asked.

Noah shook his head before the words were out of her mouth. "I tried to discourage her, but she's persistent."

"Well, you're a good-looking single man."

"I'm taken," he said.

Sam and Beth both leaned forward.

"Your divorce?" Sam asked.

"No," he scoffed. "I just found out we have a court date a week before Christmas."

"I think being separated allows you to see others," Beth said, with a knowing look at Sam.

"I'm seeing someone," Noah said, "someone else."

"Oh? It must be serious."

"I've reconnected with my girlfriend from college."

Sam sat back. Ran a hand through his hair. Sam had been the one person he had confided in over the years.

"This was a long time coming," Sam said.

"We ran into each other about a week ago at the airport in Atlanta."

"This sounds like a romantic story," Beth said.

"You can tell her," Noah said, turning his back squarely away from Abigail who was still watching him.

"Worthington made a business arrangement that required Noah to marry Claire. What he didn't know was that Noah was planning to marry…" he turned to Noah. "I'm sorry. I can't remember her name."

"It's ok. It's been twenty years. Her name is Savannah." Just saying her name out loud sent a warmth through his body.

"Noah was planning to marry Savannah."

"I handled it very badly." Noah said.

"You were young," Beth pointed out.

"No. Really badly. I just walked away from Savannah. No explanation. No good-bye. Nothing."

Beth watched him closely. "You loved her very much."

"Yeah," Noah said. "I loved her too much to watch her heart break."

"But now you're back together."

Noah nodded. "That's part of why I've made this decision. I want to be able to set my own schedule. To be able to spend as much time with Savannah as possible. I have some serious making up to do."

Sam took Beth's hand. "Sounds like they're going to have the same happy ending we have."

Over the course of the next couple of hours, Noah and Sam worked out a few details, but the deal had been sealed with that initial phone call Noah had made to Sam.

Halfway through dinner, Abigail had disappeared obviously abandoning her efforts to pursue Noah.

Noah left the restaurant in high spirits.

Tomorrow he would give his final notice to the airline.

12

"How are the children, Mary and Todd?" Savannah asked.

Dr. Smith beamed. "They're good. Todd is still at Yale and Mary is getting ready to graduate."

"Time really flies, doesn't it? Is Mary following his footsteps into architecture?"

"Oh, no. Mary is thinking about going into fashion design."

"Oh, how fun! She and her mom must have really enjoyed that trip to New York. She must have caught the fashion bug."

"I think maybe she already had a touch of it. Do you have a medication to treat the fashion bug?"

Savannah laughed. "If I had a drug for that, I'd take it myself."

"What about you? How have you been?"

"I've been good," she said.

"Still single?"

"Yeah."

"My wife's cousin is coming into town next week."

"Oh," she said, "that will be nice."

"You know she's been talking about this for a while."

Savannah knew exactly what he was talking about. She'd had dinner with Dr. Smith and his wife and they had offered to set Savannah up with Mrs. Smith's cousin.

Savannah had never given a direct answer. She didn't want to offend either the doctor or his wife. Besides, she'd seen a picture of the cousin and he wasn't bad to look at.

"Do you want me to have my wife call you to arrange a dinner meeting?"

"You know what, I'm actually seeing someone."

"Oh, good for you. Is it serious?"

"Well, it's actually kind of new. But, yes, I think it might be."

"My wife will be disappointed, but I'm happy for you. It's been a long time for you."

Savannah had a propensity to keep her social life separate from her work life. However, in an attempt to establish rapport, especially with good clients, she disclosed certain personal information. Especially clients like Dr. Smith and his wife that she occasionally met outside the office in a social setting.

She considered it to be part of the job. Considered them to be work friends.

However, it was times like this, that she regretted the need to blur those boundaries.

After the meeting, she sat in her car, jotted down a few notes regarding the meeting.

It was helpful to keep notes to remind her of details.

She firmly believed that her attention to detail was one of the things that made her successful at her job.

She checked her phone.

No message from Noah.

Reminded herself that he was working. He'd dropped her off at her house, then dashed off to catch a flight home to Ft. Worth so he could work the next day.

"Twelve hours bottle to throttle." He'd told her that was his personal rule. It meant no alcohol twelve hours before flying, but it also meant he needed to be asleep twelve hours before takeoff.

But it had been four days and she hadn't heard from him.

He had sent her a couple of quick text messages while they'd been on Mackinac, so she knew he had put her phone number in his phone correctly.

Her thoughts wandered back to those days they'd spent together and a smile played about her lips. It had been like old times, only better.

Then his words came back to her. The words he'd spoken before they left. "No strings attached."

He recanted after she'd inadvertently starting crying, but the words were there. It seemed he'd meant it.

She admonished herself for thinking that things would be different this time. That they would have something serious.

It would be a long time before she would be ready to spend time with another guy.

Being with Noah had reawakened feelings in her that had lain dormant for twenty years, but there they were, back again.

An old wound, it seemed, was the hardest to heal.

She checked the calendar on her phone. This was her last meeting for the day. Friday afternoons had gotten progressively more and more empty over the past few years as offices started closing early for the weekend. She really didn't mind.

Putting her phone away, she started the two-hour drive home.

As she pulled into her driveway, it became evident how she would spend her afternoon.

She dragged her suitcase and computer bag out of the trunk of her BMW. The house was quiet and seemed a little empty.

She tossed a load of clothes into the washer, then changed into a pair of old jeans and a t-shirt.

There were occasions when she paid the neighbor's son to clean the yard, but there were also days when she needed to do the work herself. This was one of those days.

She took a rake from the tool shed in her back yard and, after picking up stray limbs from a recent storm, began raking leaves from the pine trees that shaded her house.

Two hours later, she had several large piles of pine straw around the yard. With November around the corner, this was just the first round of required raking.

Exhausted now, she decided that she could bag the straw tomorrow. Going inside and upstairs, she ran a bubble bath in her garden tub that overlooked the backyard below. Used the jasmine gardenia scent that she always found soothing.

She checked her phone for messages, turned the volume on, and set it on the stool next to the tub.

As an afterthought, she turned on the volume and the sounds of Taylor Swift drifted through the air. After twisting her hair up and securing it to the top of her head, she stepped into the hot water and relaxed against the back of the tub.

Her thoughts were instantly filled with Noah. Seeing him across the hotel lobby in New York, handsome in his tuxedo. Sitting in his plane with his headset, deftly maneuvering them through the air. Holding her hand as they rode side by side in the carriage on Mackinac Island.

His kisses. Ah, his kisses. She closed her eyes and allowed the memory of the sensations to envelope her.

His words whispered in her ear as they snuggled on a bench looking out over the water, watching the sunset. *I missed you,* he had said.

I miss you now. Where are you Noah? Was that just a fling for old times' sake?

She'd never gotten over him. It was a hard thing to admit.

I need to let him go.

How many times had she wished for just one more night with him?

She had gotten a whole week. *I should be happy.*

Shoring up her resolve to be happy, she got out of the tub and got into her cozy fleece robe.

Went to the refrigerator, opened the door, and sighed. She should have gone to the market instead of heading home to rake the yard. Nothing in the freezer either.

She picked up her phone and located the number to the pizza parlor and called in a Hawaiian pizza.

She poured a glass of cabernet and sat on the sofa while she waited. Checked her phone. Clicked on the weather channel. There was a band of storms across the Ft. Worth area. Was Noah home? Or was he flying across the country right now?

It would have been decent for him to call.

She opened the photo album on her phone and found the selfie they had taken on the porch of the Grand Hotel.

One hand holding the camera, the other arm pulling her against him, their cheeks pressed together, both of them grinning from ear to ear. She pressed the picture, bringing it to animation. He'd captured a perfect photo. In the three seconds captured in the live photo, he turned, kissed her on the cheek, and grinned back at the camera.

She'd watched it a thousand times. Every time, it brought a smile to her face.

But tonight it brought tears to her eyes. A tear landed on her hand just as the doorbell rang. Her pizza was here and she'd lost her appetite.

The pizza turned out to be better than she had expected. With a full stomach and a glass of wine, she decided to turn in early. By the time her head hit the pillow around nine o'clock, she was sound asleep.

Her phone alarm went off at five.

Savannah checked her phone. How had her alarm been set to five o'clock?

After making sure it was off, she rolled over and closed her eyes to go back to sleep.

Five minutes later, her eyes were wide open. She sighed.

And reluctantly rolled out of bed.

This getting up early was getting to be a bad habit.

She put on her fleece robe and made a latte with vanilla syrup and creamer, her only indulgence of sweetness. Out of habit, she sat at her little writing desk and turned on her Mac computer.

But instead of pulling up her email, she paced a bit, her coffee mug in her hands.

She felt restless.

She sat back down, checked her email - mostly deleted emails, and scanned the headlines. Nothing seemed out of the ordinary.

After putting on her running skort, running top, and sneakers, she got on the treadmill and took a five-mile run in her living room via Norway - according to her iFit program.

She chugged a bottle of water and felt some better.

She had no yogurt and no fruit. A trip to the market was definitely on the list today. So, she scrambled an egg, added some cheese, and toasted two slices of bread she found in the freezer. She ate her egg and cheese sandwich while watching Fox news.

The sun was up now and she needed to bag the pine straw she had piled around the yard.

It was a bit chilly outside, so she pulled on a pair of old sweatpants and a sweatshirt. Grabbed some big garbage bags from the pantry and went outside to start cleaning the yard.

By the time she had two bags stuffed and dragged to the curb, she was sweating.

She had about three bags to go. One more and she had to

trade in her sweatshirt for a t-shirt. After the fourth, she was ready for a break. She dragged it to the curb and left it along with the others.

A dark blue sedan pulled up to her driveway. She watched as it turned in and pulled up to her garage door and stopped. Since she was on the other side, she couldn't see the driver. A little spurt of anxiety shot through her. The car was between her and the door of her house. She considered her options. She could run to the neighbor's house and call the police. The nearest neighbor was behind a grove of trees and it would take her about three minutes to jog to their front door.

She held her breath as the driver turned off the motor and the driver door opened.

And Noah stepped out.

A rush of emotions shot through her. Relief that it was someone she knew, but more importantly her heart did a little summersault at seeing him and the blood rushed to her cheeks.

That was followed by a dash of panic. She'd run five miles then gotten even more hot and sweaty bagging leaves. She badly needed a shower.

He stood on the other side of the car, watching her over it. Even from where she stood, she could see his smile.

Her feet were glued to the ground. He started toward her. She clutched the rake as he slowly approached.

He stopped three feet in front of her, still smiling.

She smiled back, her heart tripping dangerously in her chest. Did she have that effect on him?

"Hi," he said.

"Hi."

"You've been busy," he said.

He looked good. He had tucked his sunshades in his collar as he walked toward her. He had on faded jeans and a light blue oxford shirt with loafers.

Her eyes widened. This was not how she wanted him to see her. "I'm a mess," she said.

His smile widened. "Then this is a good thing."

"How could this possibly be a good thing?"

"I've seen you at your worst and I still think you're gorgeous."

She licked her lips, unsure how to respond. Did she look that bad?

"But since I know you, I'll make you a deal. You go shower and I'll bag up that last one over there."

"I look that bad?"

"Not in the least."

"You don't want to get dirty."

"He nodded toward the car. "I brought extra clothes. That is if you'll let me use your shower."

"You brought old clothes?"

He glanced down. "These are old clothes."

She frowned. "Seriously?"

"Yep."

She really wanted to shower. He did, indeed, know her well. "Ok," she relented.

He held out his hand. She put her hand in his. "I was reaching for the rake, but this is better." He pulled her into a hug.

"Alright, shower for you," he said, taking the rake.

She laughed. "I warned you."

Giving up the rake, she took off toward the house, smiling now that he wasn't looking at her.

Inside the house, she sprinted upstairs and turned on the shower. What to wear?

She stood for a moment, contemplating. Deciding the first order of business was to get clean, she stripped and hopped into the shower.

Noah was here! At her house. And he had brought extra clothes. Did that mean he was staying overnight?

Her mind raced. Was the guest room clean enough? Her sister had stayed there last. She had no food in the kitchen.

Thank goodness she'd washed her dishes from breakfast. Why hadn't he called first? Why hadn't he called at all?

How had he even found her without her address?

Noah always had been a show up kind of guy. He liked the element of surprise. He had a cell phone. A text only took a second.

She rinsed the conditioner out of her hair and gave up.

He was here.

She was happy.

No strings.

As the words came back, her good mood dissipated somewhat, but so did some of her anxiety.

No strings meant she really had nothing to lose.

She stepped out of the shower and wrapped herself in her big, cozy towel. Then went to the bedroom window and peaked outside to the side yard where she'd left the other stack of pine straw.

Noah was there, his sleeves rolled up, raking an area she hadn't gotten to. He was giving her plenty of time to make herself presentable.

She felt a little twinge of guilt having him outside working in her yard. She bit her lip. Told herself he could have called first and she would have been up and presentable for him.

Something nagged at the back of her mind, but she couldn't quite put her finger on what it was.

Going back to her bathroom, she washed her face and combed out her hair.

Took out her hair dryer and began to blow dry her hair.

Lost in her thoughts, she jumped and turned off the

hairdryer when she spotted Noah standing behind with a goofy grin on his face.

"Sorry," he said.

"It's ok. I'm not use to anyone else being in my house," she admitted.

"That's good to know."

"Yeah," she said. "You took a leap of faith."

"You did say you weren't in a relationship."

She smiled, picked up her hairbrush. "I suppose I did."

He stepped forward, put both hands on her face, and kissed her. Really kissed her. And all logical thought evaporated from her mind.

"I'm just gonna be out back," he said. "finishing up the raking. Then I'll take you up on that shower."

"Ok," she said. And watched as he turned. "Did you need something?"

"Yeah," he said. "Thank you."

A slow smile spread across her face as she listened to his footsteps going down her stairs.

Noah had just enough cockiness to make him charming.

She finished drying her hair, confident now, that they would figure out what to do next. What to do if her house wasn't exactly guest ready. What to do about her having nothing to eat. What to do about their no strings relationship.

She put on some basic makeup and went back into her bedroom to unpack – something she had neglected to do last night.

13

Noah stepped out of Savannah's shower and dried off with the towel she'd left on the counter. Her bathroom smelled like her – jasmine and gardenia.

And, he supposed, he smelled like her, too, now, since he'd just used her soap.

He smiled at the thought of smelling like a girl.

His daughter would give him a really hard time if she knew.

He went to the sink, dug around in his man bag and pulled out his toothbrush and toothpaste. While brushing his teeth, he noticed that the sink had a drip.

He would have to fix that.

He pulled on a fresh pair of jeans and a sweatshirt before wiping up after himself and, walking through her bedroom, went to find Savannah.

Walking around in her house was a little presumptuous, he would be the first to admit.

However, they had spent a great deal of time together lately and it felt, well, normal.

At least to him.

Perhaps he should ask her if she was ok with him being there.

Was it a bit too late?

He found her in her laundry room, sorting clothes and putting a load in the washer.

"Did you know you have a leak in your bathroom?"

She looked over her shoulder. "Oh yeah. I've kind of gotten used to it. I'll try to remember to call a plumber Monday. I don't really want to pay the weekend rate."

"You shouldn't have to pay a plumber for that at all."

She turned and looked at him.

"Where are your tools?" he asked.

"What kind of tools?"

"An adjustable wrench," he said, a sinking feeling in the pit of his stomach.

"I don't think I have one of those. I only have a few tools."

She pulled a basket from a shelf next to her dryer.

She had a couple of screwdrivers, a hammer, and tape measure. No wrench.

"Is this it?" he asked.

"I have some scissors and some glue in the kitchen."

"All right," he said. "I think I saw a hardware store on the way in. I'll run get what I need."

"There's no need to do that," she insisted. "I have a plumbing company that will come out and take care of it."

"You're cute," he said. "But don't you dare pay a plumber to come out and fix that faucet."

"All right," she said, pressing buttons on the washer.

He liked her calmness. Her ability to not worry about things.

He also found it charming that there were basic things she didn't know how to fix and really didn't want to know how to fix.

He always figured that if a woman could fix everything, she would have no use for a man around the house.

"I'll be back in a few minutes."

"Okay," she agreed, shooting him a quick smile before going back to sorting clothes.

He locked the front door behind him. She'd just have to let him back in. And drove the couple of miles to the local hardware store.

He purchased a wrench, some replacement washers, just in case, and some O-rings.

Back in the car, his phone beeped indicating a text message. Thinking it was Savannah adding something to his list, he picked up his phone with a smile on his face.

His smile quickly faded into a frown. It was a text from his daughter.

Daddy, can we talk?

Noah groaned and ran a hand through his hair. Conversations with his daughter were never short and simple. She took after her mother in that way

"Is it urgent?" he dictated to Siri.

Not an emergency.

He'd taught both his wife and daughter a long time ago not to contact him while he was at work unless it was an emergency.

Ever since that time he'd been taxing out on a runway at DIA and got a message from his daughter urging him to come home. She needed help.

It had taken some work, but he'd managed to turn the plane around, get off the plane, and make it home.

The emergency was a lost teddy bear.

The passengers had been told there was a problem with the engine.

Danielle had been five, but that hadn't happened again. Her mother had taken the blame for that one.

But he wasn't working today. This was a Savannah day. As he waged an emotional war with himself, he dictated to Siri.

"Can it wait until Monday?"

No response.

Noah closed his eyes and knocked his head against the back of his seat.

"I'll be home Monday. Let's talk then."

Silence on the other end.

Ok. The text came in finally.

Noah groaned and dialed his daughter's number.

"Hey Baby," he said when she answered.

"Hi Daddy."

"What's wrong honey?"

"Nothing. I just wanted to hear your voice."

"Are you ok? Any trouble with boys?"

Was that a laugh or a snort? "I'm taking a break from boys."

"Seriously? Hold on. I think I dialed the wrong number."

It was a laugh this time. "Maybe not completely, but I'm trying to get ready for graduation."

"I know, Baby, you have lots to do."

"It's a lot."

"Do you need me to help you with anything?"

"Not really."

"Ok, honey, I'll see you next week, ok?"

"Ok, Daddy."

"Think about where you want to go eat."

"I will."

"I love you sweetheart."

"I love you, too, Daddy."

Noah breathed a sigh of relief. He put the car in gear and started back toward Savannah's house.

He did not need to be worried about his family when he was with Savannah. She deserved more than that.

His mood a little heavier, he drove back to Savannah's and

stood on the front porch ringing the doorbell like any Joe Blow.

That, too, added to his foul mood.

She opened the door.

"I'll just be a minute," he said.

He went up to the bathroom and after turning off the water supply, tightened the screws and, true to his word, no more leaky faucet.

Savannah came into the bathroom, admired his work, and putting a hand on his shoulder, pressed her lips against his.

Almost like a magic spell, his black mood dissipated and he even forgot why he'd been in a bad mood to start with.

"I suppose I should have asked," he said, "if you minded if I came to visit.

"It might be a little late for that, don't you think? I mean, you've done it now. You've cleaned the yard and fixed a leaky faucet and you've been here, what, less than two hours. I think I might have to keep you."

"Is that so?" he said, nuzzling her neck.

"It is so," she said, her eyes drifting closed.

"We may have to see about that."

"Right," she said, as his lips claimed hers again.

Without taking his lips off hers, he put one arm beneath her shoulders and one beneath her knees and lifted her into his arms.

He took her to the little settee he'd scoped out earlier, purposely avoiding her bed, and sat down with her in his lap

Their lips merged, hungrily. She laced her fingers through his hair and he put one hand behind her neck, his fingers splayed on her cheek, holding her close.

She moaned softly, fueling his desire.

And reminded him of his promise to himself. Not to push her.

Not to rush things.

He pulled his lips away and held her tight against him, feeling her heartbeat pounding against his chest.

"You probably had lots to do today," he murmured against her ear.

"I did have lots to do today," she said.

His fingertips made gentle circles on her back.

"You have something planned, don't you?" she asked, her voice muffled against his chest.

He nudged her back, smiled into her eyes. Tucked her still damp hair behind her ear. "Nothing gets by you, does it?"

"What is it?" she asked.

His expression turned sheepish. "I thought we could go to the game tonight."

Her eyes widened. "Football?"

"Auburn," he said. "We always went to the Auburn games."

"We were college students." She looked askance at him. "You still go to college football games?"

"No," he said. "I haven't been to a college football game since I left here. I usually go to see the Cowboys."

"Oh wow," he felt her pull back imperceptibly.

"It's ok," he said, "I won't make you go."

She laughed and relief shot through him. "It's ok. It might be fun. I haven't been in… a really long time."

He smiled broadly. "The game starts at 3:00."

She sat up. "I really needed to do some things today."

"Ok. I'll help you. What do we have to do?"

"I have to buy groceries. And pick up my meds from the pharmacy. And dry cleaning. Saturdays and Sundays are catch up days."

"We already cleaned the yard and fixed the faucet leak. I think we're on a roll."

"Ok, then," she said. "Let me get myself ready and we'll get started. I think we can make the game."

She disappeared into the bathroom and he breathed a sigh of relief.

She hadn't rejected him.

He knew he had a bad habit of just imposing himself. Somehow it seemed so much easier to get forgiveness than permission. He'd started to call a hundred times. *Hey, how's it going? Want to spend the weekend together?*

Besides, he hadn't been a hundred percent sure he could get away until yesterday.

Savannah straightened her hair and pulled it back into a ponytail, tying a navy-blue bow to hold it in place. The bow was something she'd picked up to give her niece for her birthday, but she could easily pick up another one later. She put on an oversized gray sweater with her jeans and mid-thigh boots.

Studied her appearance in the mirror. The glow on her face could not be manufactured. Her heart was beating a little faster than normal.

She realized she was the most genuinely happy that she had been in a very long time. But she quickly decided that it was unwise to contemplate just how very long that had been.

She went downstairs to find Noah stretched out on her couch, his feet on the coffee table – no shoes. His attention focused on his iPad.

He still set her heart aflutter.

She was still amazed that he was there. In her home.

It was almost like they'd never been apart.

Almost.

"Ready?" she asked.

He put his iPad aside and, standing up, held out his arms.

She went into them.

"Thanks for letting me just barge in like this."

"Did I have a choice?" she asked teasingly.

"Always," he said, seriously.

She pulled back. "I'm happy you're here."

"Are you sure?" he asked.

"Absolutely," she said, smiling.

"Ok, then."

"Let's take my car."

She drove to the pharmacy drive-in first, pointing out things along the way that had changed since he'd been there. Things like the shopping center and the new stadium seating movie theatre.

"Are you hungry?" he asked. "We should eat lunch."

They went to a sandwich shop next. The crowd was boisterous, filled with college students and alumni getting ready for the game.

"They look so young," he commented.

"You really haven't been back since graduation."

"Not once."

The server brought their burgers and fries.

"And you never left," he said.

"I lived in Birmingham for a few years – first with my mom, then in an apartment."

"What brought you back to Auburn?"

"I always thought the lake was where I wanted to live," she said, setting down the ketchup bottle after an unsuccessful battle.

He took the ketchup bottle, got it started, handed it back.

"When I was ready to build, I just knew."

"I love your house."

"Thank you," she said. "I designed it myself."

"No. Now you're kidding me."

She laughed. "I'm not kidding. I took a basic blueprint and changed some things around."

"Now I'm seriously impressed."

"Really?"

"Absolutely. It's one more thing about you that impresses me. You're very impressive."

"I'm just ordinary."

Noah laughed. "I don't think you have an ordinary bone in your body."

She smiled. Took a bite of her burger.

What was he up to? There were so many things she wanted to ask him. So many things he would tell her when he was ready. However… if he didn't start talking soon, she would have to start asking. Perhaps there was no time like the present to start the conversation.

"Tell me about your daughter."

His eyes widened with that deer in the headlights expression that came with unexpected questions. It only fueled her determination to start asking for the information she wanted to know. Nonetheless, she took pity on him. "Does she have a boyfriend?"

"Danielle has had a string of boyfriends since she was fifteen."

Savannah laughed.

"You just think it's funny."

"Well, she is pretty."

"Having a pretty daughter is sometimes actually a curse."

"What about you? Does she have you wrapped around her little finger?"

"Of course," he said. "Though the divorce has put some strain on our relationship."

Now we're getting somewhere.

"Where did you say she was planning to go to college?"

"There are a couple of universities in Dallas that she's looking at."

"Not following daddy's footsteps?"

He scoffed. "Not at all. She's planning to major in nursing."

"That is a bit different from aviation. Does she take after her mother?"

"No," he said, keeping his eyes focused on his plate.

Ok, so obviously this was not a conversation he was ready for.

"Do you know who Auburn is playing?" she asked. Switching a conversation that wasn't going well was one of the things she was good at.

"Ole Miss," he said.

"Uh oh," she said.

"Yeah, we lost last year, but we won the previous two years."

"You have kept up."

He shrugged. Smiled. "I googled it."

She shook her head. "And here I thought you were one of those men who keeps up with his alma mater."

"A lot of people do."

"I know. Especially in a college town."

At least he was distracted now from the mention of his soon to be ex-wife.

A few minutes later, the server brought the ticket. "Who gets the honor?"

Noah took the ticket. "It seems dating has changed over the years."

"Maybe she didn't think we were dating."

"Really?" He leaned across table, put his hand over hers. "Then we need to do more things to let people know that we're a couple."

"You want people to think we're a couple?"

He smiled wickedly. "I think we make a cute couple."

Unsure what to say, she allowed him to lace their fingers together.

She most definitely had questions to be answered.

Their next stop was the grocery store. Savannah had a habit of bringing a list with her, but she'd forgot and left it on the counter. So, as Noah pushed the cart, she picked up the necessary things she could remember that she needed. She didn't have to travel next week, so she bought vegetables for salads, yogurt, and multi-grains.

"Do you need anything?" she asked as they approached the checkout counter.

"Do you have eggs?"

"I think so."

"I'll grab a carton, just in case," Noah said, and headed back to the dairy section.

"I'll wait here," Savannah said as Noah headed back to get the eggs.

The line was unusually long, but then it was game day.

As she waited, a man in his mid-forties wearing navy scrubs walked up to her.

"Savannah?" he asked.

She turned. It took a moment, but she recognized him from one of her early clinic assignments. What was his name? He was a nurse practitioner. "Yes," she said, putting on her professional smile. "Hi, how are you?"

"I'm good."

"It's been awhile. Are you still at the family clinic?"

"Unfortunately, yes," he said with a laugh. "So… you stopped coming around."

"Yeah," Savannah said. "I got reassigned."

"Oh. That's too bad. I was hoping we could do lunch or even coffee."

Savannah saw Noah coming toward her out of the corner of her eye. "Oh, well, that would have been nice. But I've got to run for now. It was good to see you."

Noah came up next to her. "I got some cheese, too," he said.

The line moved and Savannah began putting things on the counter.

"I'll see you around, Savannah," the nurse practitioner said.

"Sure," she said, turning with a quick smile in his direction. "Later."

He went to the next checkout line and out of earshot.

Noah helped her put the groceries on the counter and waited while she checked out.

Together they carried the bags to the car. Savannah didn't see the nurse practitioner again. Relieved to have gotten out of that situation, she took her place behind the wheel.

Noah had been quiet since they'd checked out.

"Who was that guy?"

Savannah didn't even try to play dumb. She knew exactly who he was talking about. "I don't even remember his name. I think he's a nurse practitioner at one of the clinics I used to go to in Birmingham."

"And he recognized you."

She backed out and pulled out of the parking lot. "I guess it's a hazard of the job."

"I have that, too, sometimes."

"Job hazards?"

"Yeah. Flight attendants. Sometimes they take advantage of access to pilots. I guess doctors do that with drug reps, too."

"Way more often than I would like."

"Do you enjoy your job?"

"I do," she said. "In spite of the job hazards."

"That's important."

He was being far too quiet. "Should we go ahead to the stadium?" she asked, checking the time.

"Sure.

"Do you?" She turned on her blinker and got on the highway. "Do you enjoy your job?"

"I like flying."

"I don't think that's exactly the question."

"No, you're right. It's not. I was waiting for the right time to tell you."

"What is it, Noah?"

"I turned in my resignation this week."

"What? Why?"

"I got a better offer," he said, with a tentative smile on his face. "This is kind of a big deal."

"I suppose it is."

"Are you going to tell me about this better offer?"

"I'm going to be doing contract work."

She wracked her memory. "I don't remember you wanting to do contract work. I mean, you mentioned it last week, but I didn't think you were serious. All I remember is you wanting to fly for the airlines."

"It seems like it's time for a change."

"Do you have clients set up? Or connections?"

He went over the highlights of his deal with Sam.

"Noah, that sounds awesome. It'll give you more flexibility, right?"

"That's the plan."

"Are you excited about it?"

"I'm a little apprehensive about leaving behind the security, but yeah, I'm looking forward to it."

It seemed like there was something he wasn't telling her, but she would have to ask him later. They pulled up to the stadium and she focused on finding a place to park.

Tailgaters were everywhere. The smell of different foods reminded Savannah of a county fair. The smells combined with the noise. People yelling. Cheering. The band was warming up somewhere in the distance.

As they made their way through the crowd to the gate, Savannah heard the cheerleaders already getting into high gear.

As they waited in line, a man about Noah's age called out to him.

Noah looked at Savannah. Shrugged.

The man, nonetheless, made his way through the crowds and stood in front of them. "Noah Worthington, right?"

"Yeah, I'm Noah. Do I know you?"

"It's me. Mike."

"Mike?"

"Yeah, Mike from flight class. We flew together."

Savannah actually recognized Mike. Sort of. He was balding now. And much heavier. But she recognized his voice and the way he stood.

She saw the moment Noah's memory clicked and he remembered him. "Mike. Yeah. It's been so long. Hey, this is."

"Savannah," Mike said, pulling her into a hug. "It's good to see both of you guys. How have you been?"

"Good," Noah said. Savannah nodded. "Good. And you?"

"I'm good. I gave up flying."

"Why?" Savannah asked. If her memory served, Mike was one of the better students in Noah's class.

"I went into the Air Force. Did two tours in Iraq and three in Afghanistan."

"Oh wow. That's a lot."

"Yeah, I just retired."

"The crowds don't bother you?" Savannah asked, remembering that most guys coming back from active service avoided crowds at all costs.

"Don't make me go to Wal-Mart," he said with a chuckle. "But I cut my teeth at this stadium. This is comforting to me."

Savannah found that fascinating. She would mention this to one of the psychiatrists she was seeing next week who specialized in PTSD. Of course, Mike may not have PTSD, but with five tours, how could he not have at least residual symptoms? Enough anyway, it seemed, to make him stop flying.

They were inside the gate now. Mike gave Noah a quick

hug. A pat on the back. "I got to run now, but I hope I see you around," he said.

"You too, buddy," Noah said. "Hey, thank you for your service."

Mike saluted him. "The pleasure was all mine." He took a step, stopped, and turned back around. "You know. I always knew you two were going to make it as a couple."

Then Mike disappeared in the crowd.

Savannah looked at Noah, but his face was expressionless. This must be their day to be recognized by people from their past.

Savannah was beginning to see the benefits of her typical quiet evenings at home. "That was kind of odd, seeing him here," she said as they walked toward their seats.

"Yeah," Noah said, still distracted. "I had no idea he'd joined the Air Force."

"He looked like he was handling it well though."

"Mike was always a good guy."

They took their seats. It was nearly time for the game to start.

"I guess you got your wish," she said.

"What wish is that?" Noah asked, looking at her now.

"You wanted people to think we're a couple."

14

Noah wasn't a big fan of college football. He had gone to a few Dallas Cowboy games over the years, but it was more of a networking thing than a love of football. It had just occurred to him that now that he was going to be relying on referrals for business, he was probably going to have to start doing a lot more of this. The idea did not exactly thrill him.

He'd brought Savannah to the game, hoping to awaken more memories of their time together for her.

Noah didn't need any awakenings. He had very vivid memories of their time together and wanted to pick up where they left off

Savannah, however, was going to take a bit more convincing.

He had to tell her what had happened with Claire. Talk more about why he had left her so abruptly.

She was being so forgiving. He hated to bring up something that might awaken old wounds. How had it been for her? Her mother had said Savannah had waited for him. Noah felt like such a cad for the way he had treated her. She'd done absolutely nothing wrong

She'd been perfect.

If she'd left him that way, he wasn't so sure he would have been all that forgiving. Would he have welcomed her back so easily? Somehow he didn't really know.

It must have been hard for her to bring up the topic of his ex-wife. Soon to be ex-wife.

He suddenly regretted bringing her here. They should be sitting somewhere with him explaining everything to her.

But she seemed to be having such a good time. Perhaps the memories of their time as college students – back when Noah had insisted they go to all the football games, were good for her. Heck, she'd built a house on the lake where they had spent so much time.

Perhaps the memories weren't painful for her like they were for him. He should really try and find out how she did it.

He returned her smile. Squeezed her hand.

He'd brought her here. He needed to get himself together. Later, after the game, at dinner, they could talk.

Then she could decide if she wanted to continue to see him. It was only fair that he give her the straight story before he spent the night at her house.

Before they got in too deep again.

Something told him, however, that it was a little late to be worried about being fair to Savannah. He'd crossed that bridge long ago.

He watched Savannah more than he watched the game. He was fascinated by her approachability. His soon to be ex-wife had also been beautiful, but in more of an ice princess kind of way.

Over the course of the game, Savannah had conversations with the woman in front of them, the guy sitting to her left, and the elderly gentleman sitting behind them. She had a way with people that he found spellbinding.

Noah was ready for the game to end. He wanted to talk to her. To clarify some things. And, he had to admit, he wanted her alone.

By the time they finally got to the restaurant, Noah was beginning to think he'd missed his opportunity to talk to her.

There was a line, of course, at the restaurant, so they waited for their table in the crowded bar. They managed to snag two bar stools and Noah ordered her a cosmopolitan and a crown on the rocks for him.

They could barely hear each other with all the noise from people around them.

"Are you ok?" she asked, leaning close to his ear.

"I'm ok," he said.

"You seem a little edgy today."

"I wanted to talk to you about some things, but there hasn't been a chance."

She lowered her eyelashes and sipped her drink. She remained quiet while they waited for their table.

Thirty minutes later, they followed the hostess to a much quieter table in the back of the restaurant.

"Will you drink some champagne with me?" he asked.

"Sure," she said. "We're celebrating your new job."

He nodded. Savannah should have become a psychologist.

He told her so.

She laughed. "No thank you. I think I've had enough school."

"You're not too old," he said.

"I couldn't afford to be a student. I have a house note, a car lease. You know, all the usual things."

The idea had wound itself into his head, though, and he couldn't shake it. "But if you didn't have all those things, you think it would be something you would consider?"

"I don't know. Maybe." She broke a piece of bread, dabbed some butter on it, and chewed slowly.

He decided to let it go for now. But he would come back to it later. "What are you in the mood for?" he asked.

"The blackened salmon with hollandaise."

"That sounds good. I was looking at that too."

The server came back and he ordered a shrimp cocktail along with their entrees.

Alone at last.

He took her hand, laced his finger through hers.

"Something's been bothering you today," she said.

"See," he pointed out. "psychologist."

She shook her head. Looked the other way. "No. I just know you."

"That's sort of what I wanted to talk to you about."

"Ok," she said, turning back, her green eyes meeting his.

Noah swallowed the lump in his throat. He didn't want to mess up what they had now while dealing with the past. But he didn't want the past to tarnish what they had now.

"I'm sorry," he said.

"For what?"

"I'm sorry for leaving you without an explanation."

"Noah," she said, her voice full of compassion.

"No. Let me say it. I was a jerk. We had it all and I just walked away."

"You had a good reason."

"No. I didn't have a good reason. I had my father. But in the end, I'm the one who did it."

"Your father pressured you."

"He threatened to cut me off from my inheritance."

Her fingers grew still. Pressed against his. "How significant was that?"

"Not worth leaving you."

"Noah," she said, searching his eyes. "What was the significance of you losing your inheritance?"

"It was a lot," he said. She narrowed her eyes. "But I didn't take any of it. At least not until after he died."

"Why? Why didn't you take it Noah? After giving up your life, why didn't you take it?"

He lowered his gaze. Felt her nail pressing into his hand now. "I didn't do it for me."

She released his hand. Sat back. Even out of the corner of his eyes, he could see the hurt.

"I did it for my mother." There. He'd never told anyone that before. He couldn't face the thought that his father might actually have left his mother destitute.

"I don't understand," she said, leaning forward again.

Noah took a deep breath and looked up. "My father threatened my inheritance, but I told him I didn't care. I told him I was going to marry you and take a job with the airlines."

Her eyes were moist now. "You did take a job with the airlines."

"I did. But I married that girl – the daughter of a business associate that allowed their companies to merge and somehow make my father richer. As a result, my father dropped the threat to leave my mother destitute."

"Would that even be legal?"

"I don't know. I didn't check it out. You met my father, but you didn't see that side of him. That side that got whatever he wanted."

He swallowed the rest of his drink. "After I got back from the honeymoon, I told my father to go to hell. I wanted nothing to do with his company or his money. And I didn't. I went to work for the airlines and lived off my own money." He scoffed. "That wasn't good enough for Claire. She took money from her father and made sure we lived up to par. She was never happy."

Savannah sat back. Her drink forgotten, melting. "You think your father would have done that to your mother?"

"No, I don't think so now. But at the time, I didn't know. At the time, I believed him when he threatened to. I don't know. I guess I thought he would leave her."

"That's awful."

"It was pretty bad. I wasn't going to do it until he pulled her into it. Then I was too ashamed to tell you. I couldn't look at you and break your heart."

Tears slipped down her cheeks. She wiped them away. "I guess if you don't see it, it isn't real," she said, with a watery laugh.

"I guess so. I was young. And dumb."

"It was a long time ago, Noah," she said.

"It feels like yesterday. And yet forever ago."

She nodded. "I know what you mean."

Their entrees arrived and both of them picked at their food.

"Did you love her?" she asked.

Noah scoffed. "How could I?"

"You stayed with her for almost twenty years. You must have felt something for her."

"The agreement was that we stay married for eight years. But ultimately it was for the child. Danielle. I stayed for my daughter. I knew that if I left, they would find a way to keep her from me."

"I'm so sorry, Noah."

"I was ashamed to tell you. Even now. I'm not proud of how it all went down."

"It wasn't your fault."

"I never should have left you."

"You didn't have a choice."

Noah pushed his plate aside. This had been a bad idea. He never should have told her about his family. He should have let the past die with the passage of time.

All he'd wanted to do was to start over with Savannah.

To begin again.

But here she was, trying to comfort him for doing the thing that had caused her so much pain.

He froze at the thought that occurred to him.

Perhaps he had been the one in pain. Much more than she was. Savannah was a resilient person. Maybe she had just moved on.

"What about you?" he asked. "What must you have thought of me?"

"I didn't know what to think."

"But you had to wonder. I mean, at what point did you figure out I wasn't coming back?"

Did he have the right to ask these questions? He didn't know.

He probably didn't even deserve to have her sitting here with him now.

But she was.

"I don't know," she said. "I looked for you, but I didn't know how to find you. That was before everything and everybody was on the Internet. You might be fortunate in that."

He barely breathed as she talked.

"I didn't date anyone. Not until I'd graduated and gone to work. I put everything into my studies. I don't think I ever really gave up on you."

"There was no one serious for you?"

"Oh sure. I was with one guy for five years. I guess he was the most serious relationship I had."

"You never got married."

"It never worked out for me."

"That's my fault," he said.

"Don't be crazy. I just spent all my time working. I didn't have time for anyone hanging around all the time."

He suspected there was more, but he didn't push her on it. Not now. Maybe not ever.

He'd done enough damage.

Was it possible for them to start over and build on the embers of what had been before?

When Savannah spoke, it was as though she'd gotten into his thoughts. "Noah, we're the same people we were twenty years ago, but time has passed. Experience has changed us, molded us into two different people. I think we have a good foundation that we can build on if we want to. But for all intents and purposes, we have to let the past go. If we're going to move forward, we both have to let it go. Thank you for sharing yours with me. It helps me to understand what happened. I needed to know. I needed to know that it wasn't just some careless thing that you did. But now is now."

"You're a wise woman, Savannah Richards."

"I'm not wise. I've just had a lot of time to think about this."

"I guess that's what I wanted you to know. I wanted to let you know that I didn't want to leave you. I needed to know if you could forgive me."

"I forgave you a long time ago."

He smiled. "Thank you."

He took her hand, kissed her palm. "Here's to tomorrow," he said.

As she brewed decaf coffee, Savannah poured a touch of amaretto into two mugs. Her hand shook a little as she poured. She and Noah had been close in college. Both emotionally and physically.

She had been young and he hadn't pressured her beyond the normal fooling around, usually with her roommate on the other side of the room. Fortunately for them, the roommate snored loudly enough that they knew when she was asleep and when she was awake.

Now that they were adults, at what point would Noah expect more? Their relationship – their current relationship, was evolving. She felt it in the way he kissed her.

She didn't know why she was nervous.

Perhaps she felt there was more at stake now.

They were no longer just a couple of college kids fooling around.

No, she mused, they were undefined.

And undefined meant no strings.

Savannah had tried the whole no strings thing. It hadn't worked for her.

She didn't know why she was so nervous. *It's just Noah.*

Noah, whom she trusted.

Noah, whom she loved.

Noah, who had a propensity to walk out of her life with no explanation.

Going back into the living area, she handed one mug to Noah and kept one for herself.

"Spicy," he said, with a wink after tasting her concoction.

"Amaretto is good for digestion, right?" she said.

"That's what my grandfather always said."

She sat next to him, their thighs touching. Was everything he ever told her engraved upon her memories from so long ago?

She shook her head.

She had been young and impressionable.

"What's going on in that beautiful head of yours?" he asked.

She chuckled.

"A whole lot of nothing important."

"Huh. A whole of something. Always."

"Maybe. Just enjoying the moment."

He glanced at her quizzically.

"That's not your enjoying the moment expression."

She laughed. Set her mug down. "Maybe I just need a little distraction," she said, as she wrapped her arms around him.

He set his mug down next to hers. "I'm nothing, if not good at distraction."

He kissed the corner of her mouth first, sending her nerve endings into electric shock. The pressed his lips against hers. Held them there until she couldn't stand it any longer. She moved her lips against his. And he responded.

He shifted her into his lap. Tilted her back until he was on top of her. He nudged her lips apart with his tongue and while caressing her cheek, tasted the roof of her mouth with his tongue.

She threaded her fingers through his hair, pulling him closer.

With one hand caressing her cheek, his other hand roamed down her arm, settling on her waist. His lips left hers long enough to linger over her cheeks, her eyelids, then back to her lips.

She couldn't get enough of him.

He shifted. Nearly fell off the sofa.

Savannah chuckled. "I think we're too old to make out on the sofa."

"Never," he said. "But I wouldn't mind if we got a little sleep... in the bed."

"All right," she said, allowing him to pull her up.

They went upstairs and Savannah paused at her bedroom door. "Do you want the guest room?"

He raised an eyebrow. "Even if I promised to be good?"

"Ok," she said, "but only for sleeping. Otherwise, we're back to the sofa."

"That's a funny rule," he said.

"I thought it was pretty good."

Nonetheless, after he wrapped his arms around her and nestled against her, Savannah was soon sound asleep.

At four a.m. Noah's cell phone rang. It was a ringtone on his phone she hadn't heard before. Pleasant, almost like Christmas music or church bells.

Noah stirred, but didn't wake up. Savannah waited, but no message came through. After a few minutes, she went back to sleep.

At six thirty-five, his cell phone rang again. This was a different ring tone. Not urgent, but not as pleasant either.

This time Noah woke and looked at his phone. He didn't answer it.

When a text message followed, he jumped out of bed and paced to the window and back while he returned the call.

Savannah kept her eyes closed, pretending to be asleep.

"Claire" he said. "What is it?"

"Where?"

"Is that all you know?"

"I'll be right there."

He went into the other bedroom and Savannah could hear him getting dressed.

She got up, put on her robe. Went into the bathroom and brushed her teeth.

When she came out, she heard Noah downstairs. The front door opened and she heard his car unlock.

A couple of minutes later, he sprinted back upstairs, stopped when he saw her standing there. "I have to go," he said. "I'll call you."

Savannah watched as he raced back downstairs and slammed the door. Within seconds, she heard his car backing out of the driveway.

Stunned, she went downstairs and checked the lock. He'd

locked the door behind him, at least. Realizing she hadn't set the alarm last night, she keyed in the code.

She stared down the driveway, but it was though he had never even been there.

She clenched her fists, then rubbed her forehead.

The grandfather clock tolled seven o'clock.

Awake, she went into her kitchen and made a cup of coffee. Then sat down at the little breakfast table in her little breakfast nook. She rarely took the time to watch the magic of daybreak. But today she watched the lake as it ever so slowly became illuminated by the rising sun.

Alone.

And unlike the sunrise she'd watched at Mackinac Island, even in her own home, the house she loved, she did not want to be alone.

Sometime. Somehow. Her heart had shifted back to once again accommodate Noah. It had been seamless. So seamless that she hadn't even noticed when it happened.

Whatever may come from here, didn't matter.

She was in love with Noah Worthington.

Always had been.

Always would be.

15

Noah sat on the leather sofa and stared at the monitors. His beautiful daughter Danielle had tubes and wires all over her body.

He watched the beeping of the monitor that told him her heart rate was ok. With each blip of the monitor, his anxiety relaxed only to increase in the next moment.

He could see Danielle's mother through the glass. Talking to the nurses. That was her way of coping. Gathering information.

Noah just wanted to hover over his daughter, and wait. Wait until she was better.

Until her eyes opened.

And she could tell him herself what had happened.

They said she attempted suicide.

Noah didn't believe it.

Couldn't believe it.

He'd just spoken to her yesterday. While he was at Savannah's. He'd said he would call her back and they could talk next week.

How was he to know that there might not be a next week?

Why hadn't he heard the pain in her voice?

Why hadn't he listened?

He reminded himself again that it wasn't true. His daughter wouldn't do that. It had to have been an accident. They had gotten it wrong. Or someone had done this to her. Heaven help the person who did this to her.

As soon as she opened her eyes and told him who did it.

There would be hell to pay.

He felt the tears running down his cheeks. He didn't bother to wipe them away.

He had a missed call from his daughter this morning. But that was something he would have to think about later.

His soon to be ex-wife came back into the hospital room. Took one look at him and handed him a tissue.

"They said she should pull through," she said.

"Should." He focused on the monitors. Everything was stable. He pulled his gaze from the monitors long enough to focus on Claire's face. "She will."

"Yes," Claire said. "She will."

"Did you know about this? That she was in emotional pain?"

"I guess I had an idea."

"Why didn't you tell me?"

"You weren't there, Noah."

"It doesn't matter. You have a phone."

"You might recall that you don't answer your phone when I call."

Noah shifted back to watching the steady beep of the monitor. This wasn't about Claire. He wouldn't allow her to make it about herself.

This was about Danielle.

Claire had found her in Danielle's bedroom. Thought she was asleep. An hour later, when she didn't respond, she'd called the ambulance.

They said they found an empty bottle of Xanax and a half empty bottle of crown… and a two liter of cola.

Noah knew the crown belonged to him or had belonged to him before he left. The Xanax belonged to Claire. Someone had exposed Danielle to crown and coke.

So, together, he and Claire had done this to her.

In more ways than one.

He scooted his chair closer and took her small hand in his. The one thing he and Claire had done right. The one thing that prevented him from regretting his marriage to Claire. The only thing.

They had a meeting scheduled with a psychologist sometime that afternoon. Whenever she made her rounds.

Just yesterday, he'd urged Savannah to become a psychologist. Was it some connection with his daughter that had him needing that from the one person he would have trusted to take care of his daughter?

Whatever it took, he would get Danielle through this. He vowed to himself in that moment, he would make it right. No matter what.

With her hand gripped in his, he lay his head on the side of the bed and for the first time in over thirty-six hours, his body overruled his mind and he slept.

Noah woke in a panic. But Danielle was still lying in the bed, the monitors beeping, her hand in his. He gently unleashed her hand and rubbed his face. Looked around.

He was alone with her. No nurse. No Claire.

He leaned over and pressed his lips against her forehead. "Wake up," he whispered. "Please wake up."

He almost promised her he'd never leave again. But Savannah…

Please, not that. Don't make me stay.

"You can come live with me," he said, his eyes tearing up.

His beautiful little girl was almost grown. By her standards, she was grown. She would be on her own soon.

Just don't die.

He took his bottle of water to the sink and filled it with water. Not up to his usual standards, but this was not his usual scene.

He drank water. Paced.

Stared at the monitors.

A young woman, mid-thirties, knocked on the door. Smiled.

"Mr. Worthington?"

"Yes," he said, taking a deep breath.

"I'm Tara. I'm a psychologist." She held out her hand. He shook her hand.

"Come in," he said, "Please take the chair."

"Let me grab another one," she said, turned back to the door and a moment later, returned with another chair.

Noah took the chair, sat it next to the one he'd been camped out in.

"How are you holding up?" she asked.

Noah shook his head. Felt the lump in his throat. "Not very well."

"That's understandable. Is there anything I can get you?"

He shook his head. Stared at Danielle.

"The doctor said it might be a few days before she wakes up."

"They told me she might not," he said, his voice barely audible.

"No one has said anything like that to me."

Her voice was soothing. Calm.

Like Savannah.

"What can I do?" he asked.

"You can first of all, take care of yourself. When she wakes up, she's gonna need you. A lot."

He turned, met her gaze.

"Are you able to sleep on that couch?" She nodded toward the couch strewn with his bag, a pillow, and a blanket.

"I don't know. I guess."

"Then I suggest you get as much sleep as you can."

"She might need something."

"If she needs something, the nurses will know."

He turned back stare at Danielle. At the monitors.

"This is not your fault."

Noah's mind couldn't let go of the crown he'd left in the house.

"You didn't know. Now that you know, you can do something."

"What?"

"She's going to need counseling. Counseling by herself, but also with you and your wife."

"We're divorcing."

"I know. But you're still her parents."

"Poor kid."

"No. She's very fortunate. I spoke to Claire a few minutes ago. She's willing to do what needs to be done. In spite of the divorce."

"I'll do anything."

"You'll need to be here for a while."

"I can do that."

Oh God. He had a new job. He had a new girlfriend. His life was crashing down around him.

Without Danielle, nothing else mattered. Not the job. Not even… Savannah. He turned his head so she couldn't see the moisture in his eyes.

"You're in a lot of pain right now."

"I just need her to wake up."

"She will Noah. Just don't give up. I'll be back tomorrow."

She handed him a business card. My cell number is on the back of this card. "Call me if you need anything at all."

He needed to call Savannah. He needed to talk to Savannah.

He couldn't talk to Savannah.

It was starting all over again.

Noah took the psychologist's advice. Tara. Interesting name. One that people would remember. A nurse had brought him a warm blanket and he had slept through most of the night, waking only a couple of times to check on Danielle.

The sun slanted across his face, bringing him to a startled awakening.

Something was different.

He sat up. On alert now.

There were no nurses in the room. Danielle lay in her bed, the monitors beeping.

He stood up, went to stand next to her at the bed. Picked up her hand.

And she opened her eyes and looked at him.

"Danielle," he said, putting his arms around her. "Baby, are you ok?"

"You're here," she said.

"Of course I'm here, Baby."

Tears leaked from her eyes.

"How do you feel?"

"Not so good. Can I get some water?"

"I don't know," he said. "I have to call a nurse. Don't go anywhere."

He rushed out the door, called, "She's awake," to no one in particular and bounced back into the room.

"There's a button here somewhere," he said, searching her wires. The nurse had shown it to him yesterday.

He mashed the button. "Somebody will come," he said. "Are you ok?"

"I'm ok, Daddy." She smiled and his heart melted.

A nurse stuck her head in the door, then returned shortly with two other nurses. They were joined by the doctor ten minutes later.

Noah watched as she was examined. He should probably call Claire.

Claire could wait. This was his moment with Danielle.

Hopefully, since he supposedly was the one who caused this whole thing, he could have a moment alone with his daughter to make things right.

After they all left, Noah went back to sit next to Danielle. "What happened, Baby?" he asked.

She turned her face away. Her chin trembled. "It was an accident."

"It's ok, Baby. We'll figure it out." He smoothed her hair back from her forehead.

She turned back. Took a deep breath. She looked so much better without the oxygen in her nose. "I feel good though," she said. "Where's mom?"

Noah took Danielle's phone from her handbag in the nightstand and handed it to her. "You call her."

It was an hour before Claire made it to the hospital room. Tara was there thirty minutes sooner.

She asked to meet with Noah and Claire alone.

Noah was reluctant to leave Danielle, but the nurse assured him that she would be ok. Besides they were just going to a room down the hall.

Tara sat facing the two of them. "How are you doing?"

"Good," Claire said.

"Relieved," Noah said.

"You're very fortunate," she said.

They agreed.

"Danielle is a very emotionally troubled young woman."

"But..." Noah said. "She's ok now."

"She tried to take her own life."

Noah sat up straight, ready to defend his daughter. "But she's ok now."

"She's very emotionally distressed," Tara repeated.

Noah felt ill. Looked toward the door. He should get back to her.

"Not at this very moment," Tara told him. "But she needs to be in an inpatient clinic."

Noah couldn't think. Tara kept talking.

"There's a good inpatient hospital in Dallas. I'll make a phone call and have her transferred there as soon as she's released from the hospital here."

"No," Claire said. "I don't want my daughter to be put in a nut house."

"It's not a nut house," Tara said. "It's a reputable psychiatric facility. They'll do a full evaluation, start her on antidepressant medication, and she'll go through both individual and group therapy sessions.

"I won't do it," Claire said.

Tara focused on Noah. "Tara will be eighteen shortly, so we'll put her in the adult unit."

"Why?" Noah asked.

"It's common for people who attempt suicide to feel euphoric after the attempt. Danielle just woke up, but I fully expect this to happen. She's already saying that she feels better."

Noah nodded. "She told me she feels better."

"After the euphoria wears off, she'll try again."

"Try again? You mean attempt suicide again?"

"Yes. And many people are successful on their second attempt."

"Oh my God," Claire said.

"I'm not saying this to alarm you. I'm saying this to let you know how crucial it is that she receive the best care possible. You want your daughter to have the best care, don't you?" Her gaze was locked on Noah.

Noah glanced at Claire. He knew Claire would fight this to the bitter end. She'd rather have a dead daughter than a daughter who was in the "nut house." This didn't surprise him. He knew the importance of social appearances to her.

"We don't have to tell anyone where she is," Noah said. "No one has to know."

"How are they not going to know?" Her voice was verging on hysterical. "They already know she's in the hospital."

"You say she's at a retreat," Tara suggested. "Or on a trip to Europe to rest and recover."

Claire appeared to consider this option.

"I know you both love your daughter dearly."

Noah nodded. "I'll do anything for her."

"Good," Tara said. "Because I'm gonna need you both to be available every day to meet with her and her therapist for the next few weeks."

Noah knew this was what had to be done. He didn't even mention his new job. He would call Sam and explain the situation. Unlike Claire, Noah did not have qualms about anyone knowing that his daughter needed help.

Tara went back to Danielle's room with them and explained her plan to Danielle.

Noah sat on the couch and watched his daughter cry and resist. "I'm not crazy," she said. "I promise I won't do it again."

So much for his hope that someone had tried to kill her. That would have so much easier to solve. Now he had no one to beat up on except himself.

After a while, Danielle realized she had no choice in the matter.

And cried herself to sleep.

Claire went to the window and stared outside.

"Can you stay?" she asked. "I'm supposed to meet the girls for lunch."

Noah stared blankly at her. He had actually married this woman. Had given her so many good years of his life.

"Before you go," he said, "we need to talk." He patted the couch next to him.

Surprise on her face, she sat. Waited.

"Let's talk about your email," he said.

"Oh that. I had forgotten all about it."

"What was that about?"

"I just thought we should stay together for Danielle's sake."

"When you wrote that, you knew she was struggling."

"I did."

"Then it really had nothing to do with you having feelings for me."

Her lips twitched in that way that meant she had so much to say, but would say nothing.

"We're not getting back together," he said.

"What about Danielle?"

"Danielle will get through this. She'll have divorced parents like all her friends. She'll get past it."

"What about…"

Noah ran his hands over his face. "What about what, Claire? What about what you'll tell your friends? Tell them you're divorced. You'll be the topic of conversation for a minute, then no one will care anymore. They'll forget all about you. Maybe you'll even find someone who meets your standard and get married again. I hope you do." He stood up. Walked around to the other side of the bed.

"Go," he said. "I'll stay here with Danielle. We'll work out a schedule when you get back so we're not here at the same time. I wish you well."

Finished with his tirade, he watched his soon to be ex-wife quietly gather up her Gucci bag and, with a flip of her blonde hair, kissed her sleeping daughter on the cheek, and walked through the door. She told the nurse good-bye as they passed in the hallway.

But no word to her husband. No thank you for sitting with our daughter while I go have a nice lunch. No wish you well, too.

Nothing.

Noah went back to his chair and sat down.

Such was the way of his life for the last twenty years.

The nurse walked in, took one look at him. "Are you ok, hon?" she asked.

Noah looked up at her. Smiled. "Yeah," he said. "Actually I am."

16

It was December 17. Saturday.

Savannah rolled over and turned the alarm on her phone off. It had gone off every Saturday morning at 5:00 a.m. since they got back from Mackinac. Savannah was very careful with her alarms on her phone.

She was one hundred percent certain she hadn't set it.

And since she hadn't set it, she didn't turn it off. Before she turned it off, she wanted to figure out how it got set to start with.

She lay on her back and stared into the darkness. Listened to the rain slamming against the window panes.

One week to get ready for Christmas. She hadn't decorated. Not that she ever decorated all that much. She spent Christmas at her mother's house or her sister's, so there wasn't really any need.

However, she hadn't bought a single gift either. That was out of character. She usually did her shopping online the day after Thanksgiving. This year, she'd sat at the computer doing some research instead of shopping.

Doctor's offices pretty much closed for the season, so she had no meetings scheduled until after the new year.

She had two weeks to do whatever she wanted.

The problem was she really had nothing she wanted to do.

She hadn't heard from Noah since the night he'd gotten the call from his wife in the middle of the night. Something about his daughter, she was certain.

Her fingers had hovered over his phone number a thousand times. She had written him little text messages a hundred times and deleted them.

The bottom line was Noah was still married. His wife beckoned and he left her in the middle of the night.

Then he didn't contact her.

For Savannah, that spoke volumes.

After a couple of weeks, she decided she wouldn't hear from him again.

She told herself she was ok with it.

That's how Noah operated.

He breezed in, upset a girl's life, then like the wind, he was gone.

Chasing Noah was like chasing the wind.

Perhaps in another twenty years, they would meet up again. Perhaps their timing would be better and they would have another go at it.

In the meantime, there was no point in worrying about it.

Unfortunately, her brain worried over it constantly. Trying to make sense of something that made absolutely no sense.

Doubtless he had family things to do.

Maybe he wasn't even really getting divorced. Maybe he just told her that to make her feel better about spending time with him.

Out of all her theories, out of all her crazy explanations, that was the one that made the most sense to her.

She'd been played.

He lived in a world of his own. A world that she wasn't part of. It was, after all, why he'd left her before.

It really was less painful this way. It just would have been nice if he would tell her ahead of time how many days she should wait before declaring him MIA.

After Mackinac, he'd shown up after a week. So, apparently a week was within range. But how long?

One week to get ready for Christmas.

Today was as good a day as any to get it knocked out. The rain was forecast to be out before noon.

She would get dressed and head out to the mall with everyone else.

If all else failed, she could get everyone gift cards.

She dragged herself out of bed, threw on a robe, and went downstairs to make a latte.

With latte in hand, she started back upstairs. She would drink her coffee and do some preliminary scouting on the internet for gifts. She had to have some kind of a plan after all.

The doorbell rang when she had her foot on the first step.

She nearly dropped her coffee and fell off the stairs.

Who could possibly be at her door at 5:30? A spurt of fear shot through her. Something could be wrong with her mother or her sister.

Somebody must have died.

Or else somebody wanted to kill her.

She inched to the door, peeked out. Noah?

She stepped back. Hallucinating.

The doorbell rang again.

"Ok," she muttered. Maybe it's not a hallucination. "Noah?" she called.

"Yeah, it's me. Can I come in? It's raining out here."

She peeked out again. Squinted. "Savannah," he said.

She keyed in the alarm code and opened the door. Noah

stood there, dripped from the rain that had drenched him. How long had he been standing there?

"What is it with you and phones?" she asked.

"I'm old fashioned," he said.

"You're an idiot." She opened the door wider, and stepped back. "Come in out of the rain."

He stepped inside. Pulled a single red rosebud from under his trench coat. Held it out to her.

She took it from him, feeling a little clutch in her heart.

Noah was her weak spot. Her drug of choice.

One look from him and she was off the wagon.

She wasn't, however, about to let him know it. "I'll get you a towel," she said, going to the guest bathroom downstairs and returning with a dry towel.

He had already shed his raincoat and shoes. "I knew it was going to rain today. Of all days."

She looked askance at him. What did he even mean? "How did you even know I'd be up this early?"

He smiled that mysteriously cocky smile that sent her heart rate into high gear. "Don't you always get up at 5:00 on Saturdays?"

Her alarm clock. Mackinac.

Seriously?

She folded her arms. "If you tell me you had this planned for all these, what, nearly two months, I'm going to…."

He grinned. "You're going to what?" He took a step forward.

She stepped backwards, but bumped up against the stair post. Then he was standing next to her, blocking her from moving.

"I hope you were going to say you're going to kiss me. After all, I had a long trip."

"You live for travel, Any excuse."

"Can't deny it," he said. "Nonetheless…"

He bent his head, pressed his lips against hers.

She moaned, leaned into the kiss. *And this is what I live for.*

He deepened the kiss and their arms wrapped around each other. She couldn't get close enough.

His cell phone rang and he jumped. It was odd. Noah was usually exceptionally calm. And rarely worried about his phone.

"I have to take this," he said, walking back to the kitchen and answering the phone.

Savannah stood where he left her. Her lips tingling from his kiss. Her emotions running rampant.

No. I won't do this. I won't allow him to keep doing this to me.

The words hurt her. Even in her head. And tears gathered in her eyes.

She dropped to the step, gathering her robe around herself. Shivering.

Felt the tears dropping onto her hands. She swiped at them. Not caring.

A few minutes later, he came back, saw her sitting there, saw the tears on her face. He rushed to her side. Pulled her to him. She didn't resist. Allowed him to cradle her against his chest as the dam broke free and she sobbed against him.

"Hey," he said, rocking her. "What is this? Sh. What is it, my love?"

Her chin trembled. She sobbed harder.

"I can't," she said, but couldn't catch her breath.

He held her, made soothing noises, and rode out the storm with her.

Savannah's pain must have been a culmination of past hurt, because the intensity was unlike any she could ever remember experiencing. She felt like she was going to explode from the inside.

She grasped at him, holding onto him for dear life.

Then, just like that, it was over.

She had no more tears.

He continued to gently rub her back.

They were both soaked now. She was soaked not only from her tears, but from his wet clothes.

She disentangled herself from him and was surprised that she still held the rose in her hand. A drop of blood landed on her robe and she saw that her hand was bleeding from a thorn.

A perfect illustration of what Noah was doing to her.

"Are you going to tell me what just happened?" he asked.

"I can't," her chin trembled. *I won't cry again.* "I don't cry around anyone else. Ever."

"I'm not sure what that says for my character," he said wryly.

"You must think I'm pathetic."

"The thought never crossed my mind."

She steadied herself. Plunged forward before she lost her nerve again. "I can't do this," she said. "I can't be your... girlfriend."

She couldn't look at him. She expected him to walk out right then.

But he didn't move.

"Ok," he said.

She looked up. The calm Noah she knew so well was back. So, he didn't care. The thought turned her tears to anger.

"You can't just come around here when you feel like it. What am I supposed to do? Just wait around until you show up again?"

"I had something to do," he said.

"We all have things to do." She wiped the blood on her robe. Handed the rose back to him.

"Look at me," he put a hand under her chin. Kissed her lightly on the lips.

She kept her face blank. At least she hoped it was blank.

"That was my daughter on the phone."

"You don't have to explain anything to me."

"My daughter just got out of the hospital last night – the psychiatric hospital."

"Oh Noah," she was flooded by remorse. "Is she ok?"

"She is now. When I was here and got that call, she was unconscious. She attempted suicide."

"Oh no. Noah." She took his hands.

"I felt responsible. She called me the day before, but I barely had time to talk to her. I told her I'd talk to her later."

"Oh, God. It's my fault."

"Not in a million years. It's no one's fault."

"You went to counseling, too."

He nodded. "She's ok now. I had to stay close for the last few weeks to go to counseling with her every day."

"Wow."

"I wanted. I needed to get through that."

"It's ok. I understand."

"I should have called you. I'm sorry."

"You had something you had to take care of."

He laughed. "Obviously another of my bad choices. But there was something else that had to be resolved before I came back."

"Something else?"

"Yes. It seems we reconnected at a bad time in my life. I needed to get it straightened out."

"And have you?"

He retrieved the bag he'd dropped at the door and sat back down next to her. Pulled out a document, about a quarter of an inch thick, bound with a binder clip at the top.

"Read this," he said.

She wiped her hands on her robe. Took the document from him.

"I'm going to make us some coffee while you read that."

"It might take me awhile," she said.

"You can skim it," he suggested. "Want to sit on the couch?"

She followed him to the couch, took the throw he offered and settled in.

She opened the document and began reading. She could see immediately that it was a divorce settlement.

"Are you sure you want me to read this?" she asked, looking up at him. This is private."

"I need you to read it. I'll be right back."

As she read, he handed her a hot cup of coffee and holding his own cup, sat across from her, watching as she read.

She skimmed a few pages, but read almost all of it word for word.

Thirty minutes later, she clipped the document back together and handed it back to him.

He looked at her expectantly. Savannah wasn't sure what she was supposed to do with this information. Did it change anything?

"You got divorced yesterday," she said.

"That was the other thing I had to take care of. Now you don't have to worry about me lying to you about being married."

"I wasn't worried about that."

"And you're not a good liar."

"Of course I am. Just not with you."

"I think that's a good thing."

"You're a wealthy man, Noah."

"I have enough to get by."

She scoffed. "You have enough to buy, what, twenty more planes?"

"Probably more like ten, but I can only fly one at the time, right?"

"Why are you showing me this?"

He moved to sit next to her. "I want you to know. I don't want any more secrets between us."

"I have some news, too," she said.

"What?"

She went to her little desk where she kept her computer and paid her bills. Picked up an envelope. Handed it to him.

He opened the letter and his face broke into a wide grin. "You're going to be a psychologist."

"Maybe," she said. "I haven't accepted yet. The clinical psychology program is full time. I'd have to quit my job and use my savings to live. It takes about six years since I don't have a master's degree yet. I have to decide if I can do that. If I want to do that."

"I think you should do it."

"Thanks for the vote of confidence, but I don't have your bank account."

He kissed her on the cheek. "It's an honor to be accepted," he said.

"You're right," she agreed. "it is."

She put the letter aside. "So what happens now, with your daughter?"

"She goes back to school. Graduates in May and goes to college."

"Just like nothing happened."

"Better than before."

"And your new business?"

"A slight delay, but it's going. I have my first flight next week."

"It sounds like you're all set."

He grinned. "As I said, I had some things to take care of."

She didn't bother to tell him that a simple text message would have made all the difference. "I didn't think I'd see you again."

He nodded. Held up his hand. "I promise to never, ever disappear on you again. If I do, you have my permission to send the authorities to look for me because it means foul play."

She laughed.

"I know you don't believe me. And I don't blame you."

"You don't have the best track record."

"I'll make it up to you."

"Ok," she said, but she knew that even though her heart was willing, her head was not so quick to jump on board the Noah wagon.

"So," he said. "In celebration of my newly divorced status, I'd like to take you to dinner tonight."

She hesitated. Hadn't she just told him she couldn't do this anymore?

"Please," he said, holding his hands under his chin. "I promise I'll have you home by midnight."

She laughed. "Ok."

"I'll be back to pick you up at 3:00. Wear something formal."

"Three o'clock?"

"Yep," he glanced at his watch. "You've got plenty of time."

She scowled at him, but he laughed and kissed her on the mouth. "Lock the door," he said, as he went outside, closing the door behind him.

She followed him to the door, which he had already locked, clicked the deadbolt, and set the alarm.

Glanced at the grandfather clock in her foyer.

She had enough time.

Energized in spite of herself, she sprinted upstairs, and ran bath water.

Comforted by the hot water, she digested all that she had learned about Noah that morning.

She didn't know if it changed anything. It hurt her head too much to even try to sort it all out.

He wanted to take her to dinner. To celebrate and she would go with him. There would be plenty of time for Christmas shopping tomorrow. Or the next day. A light week. A vacation really.

Wishing for a New York blow dry bar, she dried her own hair and put in some hot rollers for a more formal look.

He wanted formal. She could do formal.

She ate a quick lunch of grapes and cheese, then studied her closet.

There was really no choice. She had recently purchased a dress for no particular reason other than the fact that she'd fallen in love with it on sight. The sales lady had called it a mermaid dress. It was white silk, strapless, with a daring neckline. The sequined asymmetrical sash at the hip emphasized her slim figure.

Since it as too early to get dressed, she checked her email and skyped her sister.

"You look good," her sister complimented.

"Thanks." Savannah studied her sister. Charlotte rarely wore make-up and kept her hair pulled back in a pony tail. Her sister was wearing full make-up including eye liner and lipstick. And her long hair fell softly around her face. "So do you," she said, her thoughts churning. Why would her sister be dressed in the middle of the day? "What are you wearing?" she asked, straining to see what her sister wore.

"Just a t-shirt," her sister leaned back, tugged on the collar of her blue shirt. "A date with Noah?"

"What?" How could her sister even remotely know that?

"You look kind of excited and your hair is in those soft curls you only wear when you're dressing up for a date."

"Might not be Noah."

Charlotte shrugged. "Ok, then," her sister played along. "What's his name?"

"Never mind about me," Savannah changed the subject. "Where are you anyway? Why is it so quiet? Did you give the children away?"

"They're off doing their thing. Let's just enjoy the quiet moment, shall we?"

"Of course," Savannah said automatically, but couldn't let go trying to discern what was different about her sister. "Are you at home?"

"Where else would I be? I'm always at home."

Savannah checked her watch. Her sister obviously wasn't in the mood to give up any personal information. "Ok, well, I have to run. We'll talk tomorrow."

Her sister grinned. "Sounds good. Hey."

Savannah waited before she clicked off. "What's up?"

"Have fun and enjoy the moment."

Savannah clicked off and put her sister out of her thoughts. Charlotte always had marched to the beat of her own drum.

Savannah shut down her computer and went to get dressed.

Studying the finished product in the mirror, she decided she was probably over-dressed, but he'd said to go formal, so formal he was getting.

She packed her evening handbag, pulled her phone off the charger, and went downstairs to wait for Noah.

While she waited, she straightened. Shredded her mail.

Checked the window twenty times.

Wondered why they were leaving for dinner so early. Probably driving into Atlanta. Perhaps he had tickets to a play or some such.

It was easy to be full of surprises, she mused when you didn't see someone very often. She wondered what he would be like on a day-to-day basis.

You know what he's like. He's kind and funny. And considerate. And thoughtful. And ever so sexy.

Savannah sighed. The past was in the past. Right now, in this moment, her head was swirling with Noah. The Noah she knew before. The Noah who was in her life now.

He pulled into her driveway at ten minutes to three. Sat in his car for nearly ten minutes before coming to the door. She knew this because she watched him from the window.

Her breath caught as he came up her walkway.

He was incredibly handsome in his black tuxedo. She no longer felt overdressed.

She opened the door and his jaw dropped.

"Wow," he said.

"You're kind of wow yourself. I think divorce agrees with you."

"Nah," he said. "It's the company."

They went to his car, a rented BMW sedan and he helped her get inside.

"Where are we going?" she asked.

He grinned.

"You know I-"

"Don't like surprises," he finished her sentence for her. "I know you don't, but I think you'll like this one."

When they turned down the road toward the airport, it all fit together for her. "I should have known."

"You should have," he agreed. "Like you said, any excuse."

"You're incorrigible."

"That might be why you like me."

She looked at his plane as they drove up. And in that moment, decided to just embrace the fact that she liked everything about him.

She couldn't even be mad at him for more than a few minutes.

"I'm not sure I can get in the plane in this dress."

"Yeah," he said, "I should have had you get dressed when we got there. But I'll help you."

Seated in the plane, Noah did indeed look happy. And it was contagious. She could think of nowhere else she wanted to be and no one else she wanted to be with.

She was amazed, again, at the clear view from the cockpit. Surrounded by glass, it really was like being a bird.

Once they were in the air, he took her hand. "I missed you," he said.

"I missed you," she immediately responded and smiled. "I don't suppose I get any clues as to where we're going?"

"And ruin all the fun?"

It turned out to be a long flight. But the sunset was absolutely gorgeous. It gave a clue, however, to their direction. They were traveling west.

The flight was uneventful. Savannah closed her eyes and relaxed, enjoyed the sway of the plane.

Her eyes opened when they began their descent. She straightened in her seat, searching the land below. Gasped.

Las Vegas.

She turned to Noah, her eyes wide.

"It was on your list, right?"

Savannah's thoughts flew back to their conversation in Starbucks when he'd asked her to name places she wanted to visit. He'd asked for one and she'd given him five. Impressed that he had remembered, she smiled broadly into his eyes, but turned her attention to the view.

Savannah had never flown into Las Vegas at night. The view was outstanding. The lights. She could almost feel the energy from way up here.

"So is this my date to the casino?" she asked as their wheels hit the ground.

"Something like that. Since it's early," he said, "do you mind if we have drinks before we have dinner? Our reservation isn't until 6:00 local time."

She shrugged. Smiled. "I'm with you."

A limo waited for them. Savannah didn't comment, but this was certainly different from the dash and dine cars they used at the airports in their youth.

In the backseat of the limo, Noah pulled her into his arms, his fingers entwined with hers, resting their hands against her shoulder. The silence was companionable. Serene, even, after the four-hour flight.

The driver took them to the Stratosphere Hotel, then hand in hand, Noah led her up the elevator to the 107th floor to the rotating Sky Lounge. The view was breathtaking. And they were there just in time for sunset.

Once they were seated with drinks, Noah took her hand, looked into her eyes. "Are you happy?" he asked.

"Yes," she said.

"I feel so fortunate that we ran into each other again. I hope we have a new beginning."

"I thought we already had a new beginning."

He nodded. "We did." He seemed to study the view – watching the lights. Stirred his crown on the rocks.

"You're not going to drink that," she observed.

"You know I can't. But the olives are great."

She knew that Noah was firm on his twelve-hour bottle to throttle rule. And she respected that. And she knew that flying for Noah was rewarding in itself. Nonetheless, the prospect of flying all the way back to Alabama tonight seemed a bit daunting to say the least. "It would have been fun to spend the night," she said, hoping her voice sounded light.

He shrugged, kept his eyes on the view. "We can check into it if you like," he said.

What was wrong with Noah all of a sudden? "Maybe next time," she murmured and stared at her drink. He, of all people, should know that she wouldn't travel without luggage. Besides clothes, there was make-up, hair products, medication. A girl didn't just hop in a plane without a go-bag. It took all her reserve to tamp down the annoyance she was feeling at the moment. Taking a deep breath, she forced herself to look at him.

"What's on your mind, Noah?"

He turned back to her. "I'm sorry for the way I treated you."

"Like you put it," she said. "A new beginning."

They were alone in their private world, the sunset creating a glow of warmth.

"I'm sorry you've had to go through so much lately. With your daughter and your divorce."

"Speaking of my divorce," he said.

"What about your divorce?"

"I've come to the conclusion that divorce doesn't suit me very well."

A little pang of panic shot through her. "Are you thinking about getting back together with Claire?"

"Hell no."

That was a relief. "What then?"

"I'm thinking of getting married again."

"Well, you made it, what, a whole day?"

"About a day and a half, more like."

She laughed. "You men just can't stand to be alone."

"That's it," he said. "We need someone to take care of us."

"Do you have someone lined up for this marriage thing?"

"Nope," he said.

She frowned at him. "I think maybe you need time to reset after your divorce."

"You know how us men are."

"True. I have to go to the restroom, Noah."

He stood up, and she found her way to the restroom. There was a little sitting area there in the restroom. She sat on a chair in front of mirror and reapplied her lip gloss. Noah was acting strange.

Almost like he was going to break up with her. If he hadn't brought her all the way to Las Vegas…

Any excuse to fly.

She went back to the table, and Noah stood up to help her in her chair, but instead of sitting, he knelt.

"What are you doing?" she asked, her heart tripping up a notch.

"Your napkin fell," he said, picking up a white napkin from the floor and setting it aside. "I'll get you another one."

"Thank you," she murmured, taking the napkin from his hands. She kept her gaze down. Berated her treacherous heart. She closed her eyes and took a long, slow, calming breath. It's just drinks and dinner. In Vegas. The ink was not even dry on Noah's divorce papers.

Perhaps the gentle rotation of the lounge mixed with the alcohol was causing her head to spin a bit.

"Hey," he said, a mysterious smile playing about his lips.

She looked up. Answered his smile with her own.

"Why don't I call the car around to take us to dinner? But we can walk a bit when we get to the strip."

"Sure," she said. A walk sounded better than good. Some fresh air to clear her head.

Hand in hand, they went down the elevator and out to where the car waited for them.

They drove about ten minutes, then the driver stopped and let them out of the car to walk

along the crowded Vegas Strip. Hand in hand, they were engulfed by the sights and sounds of the city that never sleeps.

His hand tightly gripping hers, he suddenly stopped. People funneled around them, mostly ignoring them.

Her eyes widened and her heart tripped as he put his hands on her waist and lifted her off the ground and twirled her around. Her thoughts collided. He'd gone mad. He was ill. He was doing this right here on the strip of Las Vegas like it was nothing.

He stared at her with an intensity that blocked out the rest of the world. "Savannah," he said, not caring who heard him. "I love you."

She felt her heart open and a smile exploded on her face.

She lifted her gaze to the people walking around them.

No one had any idea how long she had waited for this moment.

For this man.

A couple, likely in their fifties, also hand in hand, walked slowly past them, the woman's eyes locked onto Savannah's. Her lips curved into a secret smile.

Savannah knew her heart was in her eyes. This woman kept her eyes trained on Savannah as she walked past. The man leaned into her, kissed the top of her head, and though she only caught of glimpse of his face, she saw the love reflected there.

This.

This was her destiny. A sense of serenity settled over her. "I love you, too."

It was going to be a late night. Again, Savannah was disappointed that Noah hadn't planned better. It wasn't like him. A trip all the way to Las Vegas seemed like it warranted at least a stay over of one night. Nonetheless, her heart was bursting. Noah had just declared his love to her in front of God and a world of strangers. She truly couldn't keep the smile from her eyes.

When they reached the MGM Grand, they walked through the casino, passed the buffet, and toward the theater to the Joel Robuchon restaurant, decorated elegantly in black and white, replete with pink tablecloths.

As she followed the hostess toward their table, an odd tingle went up Savannah's spine as she heard women laughing ahead. Noah had reserved a table in the corner with a plush cloud-soft circular bench next to the cozy fireplace with a mirror above.

When the hostess stopped in front of a table, Savannah stopped. There were three people sitting at their table. She glanced at Noah who had a huge grin on his face.

Perplexed and confused, she turned back to the women.

Looked past the gorgeous blonde young woman.

To her sister.

And her mother.

Noah stepped forward. "Emily and Charlotte," he said with a nod. Then turned to take Savannah's hand. "Savannah, this is my daughter, Danielle."

Danielle stood up and hugged Savannah. Savannah then looked into lovely blue eyes that mirrored Noah's. She had the same goofy grin that her father was wearing.

"It's nice to meet you," Savannah said automatically.

Danielle laughed. "It's nice to finally meet you too."

"Mom? Emily?" Savannah said. "What are you doing here? I don't understand."

They look expectantly at Noah.

He squeezed her hand. "I thought it was time for everyone to meet," he said, then helped her slide into the circular booth. Noah and his daughter sat on the outside. Savannah sat between Noah and Charlotte.

Dinner was a blur. Savannah struggled to wrap her head around how both her sister and her mother had ended up in Las Vegas without her knowing about it. She always knew where they were. Her mother chatted with Danielle like they had known each other forever.

"Are you ok?" Noah asked, about halfway through dinner, his lips next to her ear.

"I think so. I'm just… astounded. Why didn't you tell me they would be here?"

"I wanted to. I wanted to tell you so much that it was hard for me to talk about anything else."

"That explains it."

"It's hard for me to keep a secret," he said.

She stared into his eyes. Frowned. "How can that be? When you're so full of surprises?"

He shook his head. "I can't explain it. I guess this was just really important to me."

Before she could further contemplate his statement, they were drawn back into the dinner conversation. They were discussing a show they had tickets for that evening.

Savannah frowned. So her mother, sister, and Noah's daughter were staying the night, but they were returning home tonight. The whole scenario made no sense.

She set down her fork. "We don't have tickets," she stated. With the table suddenly hushed, she continued, fighting to keep her voice neutral. "We're flying back to Alabama tonight." She lowered her eyes and bit the inside of her lip as she battled with the emotions warring inside her. Disappointment seemed to be at the forefront at the moment.

When no one spoke, she steeled herself and looked up. All three women were staring at Noah. Savannah turned her gaze to Noah. His eyes were closed and he was squirming.

Squirming? Noah Worthington?

She picked up her glass of wine and lifted it in a toast before swallowing a sip. A bubble of laughter spilled over her lips. Noah Worthington was human. The man whose attention to details was legendary had truly botched this one.

He had brought her mother, her sister, and even his daughter to Vegas. They all had tickets and obviously were staying the night. But even though he had gotten them here all together, he hadn't thought about the two of them spending the night.

Now all eyes were on her. Eyes that questioned her sanity, but Savannah didn't care. She was going to savor the moment that Noah screwed everything up.

The server brought their ticket and Noah quickly handed the man his credit card.

He then reached into his bag, no doubt to retrieve his iPad to check the weather. Of course, they had to leave soon. Savannah's private amusement was rapidly fading.

But it wasn't his iPad that he pulled from his bag. "Since it's

Christmas, I brought gifts for everyone," he said. He pulled out three flat blue boxes and handed one each to their family members.

Before Savannah had time to react, he pulled out a fourth box, this one square all around and handed it to Savannah. She recognized the trademark Tiffany's boxes. Noted that her box was different from theirs. But it should be, she told herself. They were family members. She was his… girlfriend?

Holding the box in her hands, she looked up at Noah, a million questions swirling in her head.

"Open it," he said.

The other three women already had theirs open. He had given each of them a silver bangle which they all promptly put on their wrists.

As they oohed and aahed over their gifts, Savannah sat, silently, holding her little blue box with the white ribbon wrapped around it. Unshed tears glistening in her eyes. It didn't matter what was inside the box. It only mattered that she was here. With her family.

With Noah.

Realizing all eyes were on her again, she pulled the bow loose.

"Wait," Noah said, placing a hand over hers. "Let me." He took the box from her and removed the wrapping. Then he slid off the seat and knelt on one knee.

She swallowed thickly. Her mind refusing to function.

He took out a little blue box and lifted the lid.

Revealing a shiny, dazzling, diamond ring in a perfect Tiffany cut setting. He took her hand in his.

She gasped and lifted her eyes to his. Felt a tear drip down her cheek. Then another. She swiped at them.

What was it with Noah and tears anyway?

"Savannah Skye," he said.

Another tear.

"I've always loved you and I always will. I want to wake up with you every morning and fall asleep with you next to me every night."

She closed her eyes. Took a deep breath.

"Savannah," he said.

She opened her eyes and locked her gaze onto his.

"Will you marry me?" He reached out, wiped a tear from her cheek.

She didn't answer. She couldn't catch her breath.

Had anyone ever died while being proposed to?

"Savannah?" he asked, with a little laugh, and a nervous glance at her sister.

"Yes," she said, with a deep intake of air. "Yes," she said again, a smile breaking across her face.

Then she was in his arms and everyone at the table was laughing.

Noah slipped the ring on her finger. Put his lips against her ear. "This has been far too long coming. I don't want to waste any more time."

She nodded against his chest. Stared at the most beautiful engagement ring she had ever seen.

She was engaged!

To Noah.

The thought was almost surreal. Like he said, too long coming.

They gathered up their things and went outside.

"Where are you staying?" she asked her mother. It no longer mattered whether they stayed or left. As long as she was with Noah, nothing else mattered.

Her mother glanced at Noah before she answered. "The Bellagio."

She nodded, her hand in Noah's.

"We'll go back to the hotel with you," Noah said.

"Yeah," Savannah said, enjoying her own humor. "Our plane

doesn't leave until we get there."

They all climbed into the limo and Noah opened a bottle of champagne.

"To us," he said, holding up his glass.

"I'm so glad you all could be here," Savannah said, then found herself fighting back tears again.

They clinked their glasses together and sipped champagne while until they approached the front drive of the Bellagio.

They all got out and went into the lobby.

Noah stopped, and turned to face Savannah. Held both her hands. "There's one other thing."

Savannah couldn't imagine what else Noah could possibly have on his mind. They had just gotten engaged. Perhaps he wanted her to move with him to Ft. Worth.

These were things she hadn't considered. She loved her house. She was thinking about going back to school.

She must have had that deer in the headlights look on her face.

"Savannah," Noah said. "Stop thinking."

She mentally shook herself. Smiled.

She was engaged to Noah Worthington.

"We're actually staying here tonight."

"I don't have…"

"I know," he stopped her before she could explain, again, that she needed her go bag.

"Your mother brought everything from her house. Your make-up. Some clothes."

Savannah looked her mother who merely shrugged. "It's what he wanted. I didn't think you'd mind."

Her thoughts were too jumbled for her to decide if she minded or not. Then it struck her. Champagne. Noah had drunk champagne in the limo and wine at dinner. He'd planned this all along. So much for Noah missing details.

"Ok," he said. "There's one other thing."

She laughed. She couldn't help it. "What?"

"Remember how we were never friends?"

"Of course," she said, smiling at the memory of the way he had kissed her on their first date.

"I don't want to be engaged either."

He'd gone mad.

Again.

"I don't understand," she said, feeling the weight of the diamond on her finger.

"I want to be married."

"Ok," she said.

"Now," he said, a mischievous smile on his face.

"Right now?"

"Sure," he said. "Everyone we care about is here."

Savannah looked at her mother and sister watching them expectantly. His daughter, a smile on her face.

Almost on cue, the wedding march wafted through the air.

I'm hallucinating.

"And," he said, taking a step back to look at her. "You're wearing white."

Savannah laughed. "What are the odds?"

"I think I hit the jackpot."

Noah had set up everything through the hotel and all the details had been handled.

She had flowers. There was a cake. A photographer.

The rest was a hazy jumble. They had skipped the whole friendship stage and they had breezed past the engagement phase.

Thirty minutes later, Noah's lips were on hers and she was Mrs. Noah Worthington.

And just like that, twenty years were gone in an instant.

"We did it," he said.

"I had almost given up on you," she said.

"Key word, my love," he said against her lips. "Almost."

EPILOGUE

TWO DAYS LATER

The line to fly out of Vegas was long. They sat quietly waiting their turn for take-off. Savannah had run out of small-talk and Noah didn't seem particularly chatty.

Two days had passed since the wedding and Savannah still glowed when she looked in Noah's direction.

If she had thought they were close before, they were even more close now. Bonded in every way.

After sitting quietly for a few minutes, she asked, "When did you first know you wanted to be a pilot?"

"The minute my father sat me in the captain's chair of his private plane."

"Really? How old were you?"

"Four."

"You've got to be kidding. Four years old?"

"No kidding." He looked around. "It was at night sort of like this," he said. "Crowded."

"What was he thinking?"

"I don't know. Bored maybe."

"Are you? Bored?"

"Me? Never when I'm flying. But being a passenger can definitely get to be boring. Are you?"

She shook her head. Not bored. Concerned about Noah's suddenly quiet mood.

"You know what?" he said, unbuckling his seat belt. "You fly."

"What? No. I don't know what to do."

"I'll help you."

"I can't Noah. It's not safe."

"Of course it is. I have my own set of controls." He nodded toward the controls in front of her.

He reached over, unbuckled her belt.

They changed places and got buckled back in. Savannah's heart raced. Noah had indeed gone insane.

She was still holding her handbag. Looking around for a place to put it, she saw a side pocket. Her slim handbag slipped right in. She grabbed the wheel and held on.

Noah laughed.

"You don't have to hold it yet."

"Come on, Noah, you get us in the air first."

He must have seen the panic in her face because he acquiesced.

And got them safely in the air.

After the plane leveled out, he switched the control over to her.

"Your turn," he said.

Savannah's eyes widened.

"Put your hands on the wheel and turn ever so slightly."

She did. And the plane responded. "Oh no!"

"You did that. Now turn it back."

She gently eased it back on course. "Wow. Now what?"

"Now you just sit back and hope nothing weird happens."

"Noah!"

"If anything weird happens, I'm right here."

"Did your daddy let you fly?"

"Oh no. I was back in the back before takeoff."

She cut her eyes at him.

"That was different."

"Should we be watching for other planes on the... air?"

"An alarm will go off if radar picks anything up."

"Cars should have that."

"Agreed. But it wouldn't take long to be become desensitized."

"Hmm."

Her lips felt a little dry, so she reached with one hand for her handbag to get her lip-gloss out. Instead, her fingers brushed against a little flat box.

Keeping her eyes on the air in front of them – from driving habit probably, she pulled out the box. A blue Tiffany box tied with a white ribbon.

She stared at the box. Looked at Noah who watched her.

"Noah."

"I told you I was thinking about taking a wife."

She examined her hand. "I think you already did that."

He winked at her.

"So, what, the first girl who comes along... you'll be ready?"

"Merry Christmas, ma chérie," he said.

"Wait," she said. "When did you buy this ring?"

"I bought it in New York. The day of your presentation. While you were out shopping, I

went shopping, too."

"How do you know I was shopping?"

"I know you, remember?"

She laughed. "Who's this one for?"

He smiled into her eyes. "I think it might be for my wife?"

He opened the box revealing a silver bangle similar to the

ones he had given her family and his sister, but this one was actually two, perpetually interconnected.

"I was thinking about that. I might have a condition about marrying you."

"You already said yes"

"You didn't give me time to think."

"All right. What's your condition?"

"That you not disappear on me again."

"I vow right here, right now, to never again go anywhere without letting you know."

She smiled. "That might be a little bit excessive. We'll have to figure that part out."

"I love you, Savannah Skye," he said, putting his arms around her into an embrace, nestling her head beneath his chin. "I have from the very first day we met. It was always you."

And he had always been the one for her. She'd been waiting for him her entire adult life.

And flying high above the world, with no one there but the two of them, she had a glimpse into their future. That life with Noah Worthington would never be dull. It would be exciting and comfortable all at once.

And her heart had found its home.

And this time around…

This time it was forever.

❧

Loved Reading about Noah and Savannah?
How about a Short Story?

GET MY BONUS SHORT STORY
https://BookHip.com/JJGCQCQ

ARE you ready for Claire's story? Read the next sweet second chance story in the For the Love of the Flight Standalone Series.

Turn the page for a preview of Love Again…

KATHRYN
KALEIGH
love
FOR THE LOVE OF THE FLIGHT

PREVIEW LOVE AGAIN

Claire Worthington believed that life moved in only one direction. Forward.

"Mom!" Danielle said excitedly as she approached Claire down the wide UCLA hallway. "My psychology class is so lit. The instructor is on fire."

Claire gathered up her iPhone and iPad, drew her handbag over her shoulders. She'd been waiting for two hours for her daughter's classes to end. "So... you like it?" Claire asked for clarification.

Danielle grinned. "It's gonna be awesome."

"That's great," she said. Claire glanced at her watch. She had just enough time to get Danielle to her counseling session at Resolutions Treatment Center, then they could have a quick lunch before Claire's meeting with a new artist coming in at two o'clock.

They walked together down the hall at UCLA, dodging students hurrying to their next class, most of them looking down at their phones.

"He runs the Psychology Clinic, so he's gonna let us observe some sessions. Can you believe it? It's my first semester and I already get to observe."

"That's great, honey," Claire said. Ever since Danielle began mental health treatment last winter, she'd been dead-set on studying psychology. She'd been so disappointed that her hospitalization had caused her to drop out of her advanced classes in the spring, that Claire had pulled some strings and gotten her into summer classes at the university at the last minute.

Scheduling had been an utter nightmare ever since. Spring had been a process of Danielle finishing up high school in Ft. Worth and moving to Los Angeles. Fortunately, Claire already had a house in L.A. Considering everything that had happened in the last few months, the move had gone smoothly.

Since Claire had to attend mental health counseling with Danielle twice a week, Claire drove her to class those days.

"Grayson is even going to have an art therapist come talk to us so we can see what that's like."

Claire stopped and gazed at her daughter, causing the other students to flow around them.

"Mom, what?" Danielle had that panicky *Please don't let the other students find out I have parents* look on her face. "Come on."

Claire followed, but her brain remained frozen. The art therapy part was interesting and Claire wanted to hear more about it. Later.

Something else entirely had her attention, however, at the moment.

Grayson.

A name that was becoming more popular with babies born today, but quite unusual during Claire's generation. She knew because she'd looked it up.

Did she dare ask?

She had to know. "What's his last name?" she asked, holding her breath.

Danielle shifted her backpack and smiled as she checked an incoming text. "I don't know," she said, keeping her eyes on her phone. "Can we skip therapy today?"

"No," Claire said automatically, exhaling in frustration. Danielle asked the same question nearly every day. Today, however, her daughter was particularly glowing. The psychologist had warned her that Danielle would have fleeting moments of happiness. But that had been months ago. Surely at some point she no longer had to worry when her daughter was happy.

"What did he look like?" She asked.

"Grayson?"

"Yes. Shouldn't you call him Dr. or Mr. or something?"

Danielle rolled her eyes. "It's not the south, Mom. It's L.A." Then she stopped texting and looked up at her mother. "Cute," she said. "About Daddy's size. Your age maybe. I don't know. Do you want me to find out if he's married?"

"Heavens no!" Claire said, feeling the flush on her cheeks.

"Why do you want to know?"

"I had a friend in high school named Grayson. But it couldn't possibly be the same guy."

Danielle shook her head and attached her gaze back to her phone. "No way. He wouldn't have been your type. This guy just retired from the Air Force."

Claire clasped a hand over her mouth to keep from gasping. Grayson Moore had been in the delayed entry program and entered the Air Force the day after graduation. He'd promised to write, but he hadn't. Not even once. Not one letter. Not one phone call. It was twenty years ago, so they hadn't had cell phones. Well, Claire had a cell phone, but Grayson didn't. Grayson hadn't had email either.

She sighed as she steered Danielle, whose attention was glued to her phone, her fingers flying over the screen, toward the car. Things would have been so much different if they'd simply had cell phones back then.

The name and the Air Force part matched up, but a psychology instructor? Claire tapped her fingers on the steering wheel as she waited for traffic to move.

That didn't fit. Not even a little.

DANIELLE'S THERAPY session was uneventful. Danielle seemed to be truly excited to be starting college. Her daughter had just gotten back from spending a week with her father Noah and his new wife. Claire and Noah been divorced just over six months. Noah had gotten married the day after he and Claire had officially gotten divorced. Talk about not letting the ink dry.

But Claire was happy to have it over with. Now she didn't have to worry about the obligatory visits to Ft. Worth to be with her husband.

Claire had a house in L.A. and a growing business. She'd been growing her business for years, but her husband had no idea. He thought she was here sipping mimosas with her girlfriends.

Technically, she began to network before she even married Noah. By the time they were married, she was having business meetings several times a week. Throughout the early part of their marriage, Noah thought Claire was taking money from her father to supplement Noah's income. She never told him the truth. She'd been earning the money and never once touched her father's. Well, that didn't include the start-up money her father had given her, but Claire didn't count that since she'd paid it off in mere months.

After the session, she and Danielle drove back toward the university and had lunch at a trendy little restaurant set up in the middle of a greenhouse. Claire ordered a fried green tomato po'boy with avocados, and veggie bacon and Danielle ordered a shrimp po'boy. If the two of them had a favorite restaurant to go to together, it would have to be this one. It was called the York and Orleans and they both had favorite lunch items on the menu.

Claire was sending an email on her phone to a vendor to begin discussing wine options for an upcoming fundraising event. As she hit send, she noticed that Danielle had uncharacteristically set her phone down on the table and was staring across the crowded restaurant.

Though Claire glanced in that direction, she didn't see anything out of the ordinary.

Then she heard his laugh.

Every nerve cell in her body tensed.

And a memory from twenty plus years ago was awakened.

"Mom?" Danielle whispered. "It's him."

"It's who?" She whispered back, but her eyes were glued to the handsome man in the white shirt and black slacks three tables over. He sported two-day old stubble on his face and his hair was still thick and dark.

Tall, dark, and handsome.

That's always how she'd thought of Grayson Moore. Now he was even more handsome with twenty years of maturity on him. If she hadn't heard his laugh, she probably wouldn't even have noticed him. Well, she would have noticed him, but she wouldn't have recognized him.

"It's Grayson," Danielle said. "My psych teacher."

No. Way.

"Come on," Danielle said. "I'll introduce you."

Grayson was with another man, a student perhaps? Or a younger colleague? "No," she said, but Danielle was already standing up and walking toward his table.

Claire was in full panic mode.

This couldn't happen. Not like this. She got up and walked the other way. Toward the restroom. She needed a second. Just one second.

Claire Worthington didn't panic.

KEEP READING Love Again…

Kathryn Kaleigh is the author of over seventy novels, over one hundred short stories, and many collections.

kathrynkaleigh.com

www.ingramcontent.com/pod-product-compliance
Lightning Source LLC
Chambersburg PA
CBHW030339310726
48979CB00001B/97

* 9 7 8 1 6 4 7 9 1 3 9 7 7 *